ECHO CHAMBER

Geonn Cannon

Supposed Crimes LLC • Matthews, North Carolina

This book is a work of fiction. Names, characters, places, and incidents are products of the author's imagination or are used fictitiously. Any resemblance to actual events or locales or persons, living or dead, is entirely coincidental.

All Rights Reserved
Copyright © 2024 Geonn Cannon

Published in the United States.

ISBN: 978-1-952150-46-3

www.supposedcrimes.com

This book is typeset in Goudy Old Style.

ECHO CHAMBER

The first time I saw Darwin was the day he punched me in the face.

Technically the first time I saw him was *after* the punch. I never saw him coming. I was twenty-two, standing on a street corner in Chicago. waiting at a crosswalk when someone jabbed me in the shoulder. Hard. Two fingers. Jab. Jab. I turned to see who it was, and bam. Fist. Nose.

I don't know if you've ever been punched in the face, but it's a whole body affair. My arms flailed out, trying to protect, deflect, and defend all at once but only succeeding in dropping my coffee. My legs went rubbery and I dropped straight down on my ass, like a toddler still learning the finer points of walking. I put both hands over my nose and looked up to see what the hell had just happened.

Darwin stood over me, eyes filled with rage. He leaned down to jab a finger at me. I flinched. "You know you had that coming," he said. "Consider us even."

Then he turned and stormed away, shoving away the two bystanders who tried to detain him for assaulting me. Three other strangers were crouched down around me, asking if I was okay, if there was anyone they could call. I told them no, I was fine, even though my nose had started bleeding by that point. I told them there was no reason to call the police, I was fine. Well, I was bleeding. But I was fine. I just didn't want to waste the day making a police report. Trying to pretend like it was just a random attack. It might have seemed that way from the outside. But even if I didn't know the whole story, I knew *myself* well enough to take Darwin at his word.

I wouldn't know why Darwin punched me until sixteen years later, when *he* saw *me* for the first time.

And you know what?

I kind of *did* deserve it.

PART I
ME MYSELF AND I

CHAPTER ONE

I was born at 1:02 am on a Saturday morning. I know because I was there. Well, obviously I was there. But I visited the day some twenty-six years later, so I can confirm the exact time.

I like hospitals when it's early. Visiting hours are over, so everything is quiet and you realize how wide those halls are. Usually half the lights will be off so the patients can sleep, and that casts cool shadows on the walls. The only people around are preoccupied doctors, who wouldn't be there this late unless it was an emergency, and nurses who are too tired to talk at the nurses' station. Everything is quiet enough you can hear their shoes squeak on the tiles that have very recently been polished to a shine by the janitors.

Hospitals are pretty easy to sneak into. You just have to walk with purpose, like you know exactly where you're going. Actually, I've found that works with a lot of places. If you look like you're in charge, people very rarely challenge you. The trick with hospitals is you also have to look distraught. Thousand yard stare, heavy breathing, it's helpful if you can conjure up a few tears. Someone might scold you about visitor hours, but if you look upset enough, they usually won't push too hard.

I didn't run into any opposition the morning I was born. I made my way to the maternity ward and stood in front of the nursery's big glass window. I thought that sort of thing only existed in movies and TV shows. A nice cinematic way to show the characters pointing at the baby that would kill their show. It was vaguely unsettling in person. Like a display cage at the zoo. They should have put up a sign: *Come down the hall, stand in front of the glass, look at all the new humans that have arrived today.*

I shared my birthday with four other babies. The five of us were lined up right in front of the window, and I was the one in the middle. I had been standing there for a few minutes when baby-me opened her eyes and stared directly up at me. No hesitation, no obvious confusion, almost like she knew I would be there. And maybe she did. Who knows how this bizarre talent of mine works? I leaned closer to the glass and narrowed my eyes at her. Her lips twisted into a weird rose petal, and I couldn't help but feel like I'd been insulted.

"You looking at me, baby?" I whispered. "You think you're so hot. Can't even walk. Well, enjoy it while you can, baby."

She, of course, didn't respond.

The squeak-squeak-squeak echo of shoes announced the approach of a nurse. I straightened up and put my hands in the pockets of my leather jacket, trying to act like a normal person. A normal person who was looking at newborns in the middle of the night. I'm sure there are weirder hobbies.

"Good morning." The nurse's voice was chipper but she kept her volume low. She stopped next to me, and I had to fight the urge to groan. She was young, maybe directly out of nursing school. Her scrub top had clowns and puppies on it, which seemed like a very odd combo. "Which one is yours?"

I pointed at my baby self. "My sister's."

"Oh, she's precious." She looked at the baby, then at me. "She has your chin."

"Yeah. It... runs in the family."

The nurse chuckled. "Apparently. Would you like to hold her?"

"No," I said, way too quickly. "Uh, no. I think it's probably better to let her sleep."

"Probably," the nurse said. "Well, let someone know if you change your mind." She touched my arm and leaned close like she was sharing a secret. "Babies love to be held. It's very good for them."

I nodded. "I'll keep that in mind."

She wished me a nice day and continued on her way. See what I mean? People assume you belong. Nine times out of ten, it's easier than making a fuss or arguing with someone.

When she was gone, I looked at the card on the front of my bassinet. Name, weight, time of birth, etc. I assume most of the information was correct. "Chloe" was right. But it said my last name was "Cross." I guess it's technically true. It's the name my mother gave them. It's just not a name we shared.

At the bottom of the ID card, there was a room number. 604. I took a deep breath, looked around to get an idea of where the six-hundred block might be, and started walking in that direction.

I followed the signs on the wall until I found it. 604, with a white board over it that said EVE CROSS. A fake name, provided by a fake driver's license, allowing my mother to vanish into the wind after bringing me into the world. The door was half open and there was a light shining inside. I paused on the threshold and peeked in. The light was coming from beside the only occupied bed, where the patient had fallen asleep with an open book on her chest. The window shades were drawn. I stepped inside and closed the door before any other errant nurses could intercept me.

And just like that, I was alone with my mother.

I stared at her. I hadn't really come to this visit with a plan. Had I been hoping she would be awake? Or was it ideal that she was asleep? So I could take a breath to deal with the enormity of this moment? So I could just take her in without worrying about what I'd say, or what she'd say. She was Asian, which I'd always known about, even though my father must've been white. I kept my hands in my jacket pockets. She didn't move, didn't twitch. She looked utterly drained, as if... well, as if she'd just pushed another human being out of her body a few hours earlier.

I stepped quietly to the bed and moved one of the two guest chairs so it was facing the same way she was. Looking at her was a bit too much. Sitting beside her was almost too much. Much too much. I balled my hands into fists, then flexed my fingers. I remembered the little baby fingers I had just seen in the nursery. They'd grow up to be these fingers. Amazing.

In about four hours, she would leave this hospital with me in her arms. She would carry me to a park, where she would sit with me on her lap for half an hour, according to the people who talked to the police later on. When she got up, she would place me on the bench and walk away. And that would be the end of her mothering career, at least as far as she was concerned.

She murmured something and her body shifted under the blanket. I glanced over, casual-like, the way you'd look at the person next to you on the subway. She put her hand on the book to hold it in place and blinked at the foot of her bed. I stayed still until she turned her head in my direction. Her shoulders jumped a bit when she realized I was there, then she sat up straighter and rubbed her eyes into focus.

"You don't look like a nurse," she said, her voice slurred with sleep.

"No. I'm just visiting."

She looked harder at me, still squinting. "Do I know you?"

"No," I said. "No, you don't."

Her eyes widened. Suddenly she seemed much more awake. "Chloe?"

I turned toward her, shocked enough by what she said that I couldn't speak. I stood up from the bed and put a little distance between us.

"Why would you guess..."

"It's not a guess. You are, aren't you?" She looked me up and down, appraising me. "Is this the first time you're visiting me?"

"I-I don't..."

"I'm sorry." She pressed her lips together and looked down at her hands. "I know what happens next. And I can imagine how you feel about me. But if I don't get another chance to say it, I want to say it now. I am very sorry for whatever you go through between today and..." She waved her hand in my direction. "Whenever you are."

I shook my head. "I can't do this. I don't know why I thought this was a good idea. I need to~"

And then the room was bathed in late afternoon light. A different woman was in the bed my mother had just been occupying. She was preoccupied by the swaddled baby in her arms, but something about my arrival made her look up.

"Oh! My goodness!" She laughed and shook her head. "Sorry, I'm just... Sorry. Uh. I didn't even hear you come in."

"Wrong room." I held up a hand in apology as I fled.

The hallway looked mostly the same as it had when I went into the room. A new coat of paint, and of course more crowded since it was later in the day. I started moving fast, not running but at a steady clip that made people instinctively get out of my way. I glanced at the clothing of visitors I passed. I took note of the fact some of them had smartphones. That was a good sign. Comforting. If I wasn't back on home ground, I was somewhere close to it.

An older nurse stepped out of a room directly in front of me. I had to trip over my own feet to keep from colliding with her, but fortunately saved myself before I fell. She put her hands on my shoulders to steady me.

"Whoa, nellie! Posted speed limits are..." Her face twisted in confusion. She pulled her head back to get a better look at me. "Hey. I've seen you before, I think."

I looked into her eyes and immediately knew she was the young nurse who had stood outside the nursery with me. Her scrubs were still decorated with clowns and puppies, but they'd gone up a few sizes since the last time I'd seen them. I smiled awkwardly and stepped around her.

"I think I just have one of those faces."

"No, wait, I meant I remember that jacket..."

I left her behind me and didn't slow down again until I reached the lobby. Hospitals might be easy to sneak into, but even their security would investigate if someone went running out the door at a full sprint. I moved as casually as possible through the sliding doors and stopped on the sidewalk to scan the parking lot. I didn't have my phone on me, which was a stupid oversight. Normally I could just turn it on, it would connect to the... Cloud? Satellites? Google? It would connect to whatever entity runs the world in the modern-day and update the time appropriately. Without it, I didn't have an easy way of confirming when I'd landed. Time traveling was much simpler during the era when newspaper stands were planted in front of every business. Just a quick glance could tell you the exact day and year. No awkward conversations. No Sherlocking.

I went to the first row of cars and looked at their license plates. 2024. Good, that was excellent. Right where I wanted to be.

Home.

Unfortunately, I had no idea what day or month it was. And I had no idea where I'd left my car. I took out my wallet and checked to make sure I still had my Ventra card. Fantastic. I could at least get somewhere with more information.

The nearest El station wasn't far. Now that I'd gotten my bearings, I knew the city well enough to walk the entire way on autopilot. I climbed the stairs, waited on the platform, and found a seat without leaving the comfort of my wild swirling thoughts. All I could think about was the day I was born. Seeing my mother for the first time. Actually looking into her eyes and hearing her voice. I'd prepared myself for that, or at least I thought I had. Maybe that was part of the shock I was currently experiencing. My hands were shaking in my lap. I stared out the window but I could really only see my reflection. I thought about the baby me, back in that nursery, also looking at a sheet of glass, only seeing herself.

I was the first face I ever saw. That's a strange thing to know.

But not as strange as the fact that my mother had recognized me. And not only that, she knew.

She knew I was a time traveler.

I've never known why or how I can jump through time. It took me a few trips to realize that was even what I was doing. When I was a kid, I just assumed that sometimes buildings could pop up overnight and just as quickly disappear. The cities where I lived were constantly in flux. The first time I knew something wasn't right was when I came out of my bedroom to find my foster father sitting at the breakfast table, much grayer than he'd been when I went to bed. He dropped his toast, startled enough that he didn't even look down when it bounced off his leg and hit the floor.

"Chloe?"

He looked so confused. I can only imagine what he thought. From his point of view, the little girl he'd fostered for ten months had just walked into the room looking exactly the same as she had twenty years earlier. He started to stand up, then called for his wife. I didn't know what was happening but I had a feeling I was about to get into trouble. So I thought about leaving. I thought about it Very Strongly.

Then he disappeared. The new dining room table changed back to the one I recognized. It was still morning, but my foster mother was in the kitchen making oatmeal. I could smell the brown sugar so strongly that it was impossible to believe it hadn't been there a few seconds ago.

"Morning, dear," she said. "You're right on time."

But I've never been on time in my life. Not after that moment, not really.

I closed my eyes and let the train rock me into a light doze.

I'd always fought the urge to go back and meet my mother. I expected the rage to take over, or that it would be too sad. Part of me understood why she would leave a baby on a bench. Another part of me wondered how the hell she could possibly have just abandoned me like that. I'd spent my entire adult life wavering between being terrified of what I would find and eager to just get it over with. Quick like a band-aid. I always lived right on that edge. And there was the fear that, once I'd done it, it would be over. No more speculation, only answers. Hard truths I would have to accept and process and live with, no hope.

There was no big "AHA!" moment that finally made me do it. I was just riding the bus when I saw a kid sitting on his knees, watching the city go by outside the window, and his mother was pointing out the buildings they passed and telling him what they were, if she knew, or making things up if she didn't. That was all it took. Just a mother, like hundreds of others I'd seen, and I suddenly *had* to know. The hope wasn't worth it. The speculation wasn't worth it. I knew where to find my mom, and I just had to take myself there.

I went. I met her.

And now I knew that she knew I was a time traveler. She knew my name. But she hadn't named me. So how could she have—

My eyes opened.

Is this the first time you're visiting me?

"Son of a bitch," I muttered, sitting up straighter.

I was going to visit her again, apparently.

Well. That was something to look forward to. Or dread.

Most likely dread.

When the train reached my stop, I rushed to be the first one out the doors. I didn't know why I was in such a hurry to get home. Maybe I just needed to anchor myself in a familiar place, in my actual real time. I needed something solid that I could be certain of.

I lived close enough to the station that the train rattled my windows when it passed, so it was only a quick jog before I was fumbling with my keys and slipping into my apartment. I pressed my back to the door, took a deep breath, and let it out slowly. Safety. Certainty. And...

My apartment didn't smell right.

It didn't smell *bad*. But something was cooking. I pushed away from the door and took a few steps forward, craning my neck to look around the wall that separated the kitchen from the living room. I didn't want to run into myself. Not today. I couldn't handle it after what I'd just been through with my mother. But I - she - would've heard the door open and shouted a hello. It's what I usually did when I heard an unexpected door close in my house. Common courtesy to my other selves.

The woman was at the stove with her back to me. Her hair was loosely pinned up, a dirty blonde explosion with strands going in every direction. She was stirring with her left hand, her right resting on her cocked hip. She was in jeans and a sleeveless top, and I could see the tie of an apron at her neck and waist. She was humming quietly, but she stopped when she sensed me looking at her. She turned and smiled, raising an eyebrow.

"Hi," she said.

I smiled in a way I hoped looked natural. "Hey."

She lowered her voice to a whisper. "Why are we lurking?"

"I didn't know if you heard me come in. I didn't want to startle you."

"Well, sneaking up on me is definitely the way to avoid startling." She turned back to the stove. "I'm almost finished here. Do you want to get the bowls and silverware?"

I cleared my throat. "Actually, uh. Yeah. I'll do that. But actually, I need to clean up first."

"Okay." She nodded without turning around.

"I'll be right back."

I went down the hall to my bedroom. So I was a little bit off about when I'd come back. Not my actual time, but a few weeks or months ahead of when I left. And in that time, I had apparently met someone. And we'd gotten serious enough that she was making me dinner. The thought was kind of exciting. Like seeing a preview for a movie you're really excited about. It was no big deal. I was always getting sneak peeks of things from my life. Rarely future peeks, but they weren't unheard of. I always had calendars around, and I was meticulous about keeping them up to date for situations just like this.

I went to the end of the hall and stepped into a complete stranger's bedroom.

Not my bed, not my bedding, not my clothes draped over the chair by the closet door. Something huge had happened, something bigger than a slightly-serious relationship. For the bedroom to have changed *this much*, I would have to be living with her. That didn't seem possible. Not if it was still 2024. I wouldn't take a step that big in such a short amount of time. This was... domestic.

"What the shit," I muttered, moving deeper into the room.

We'd bought a bed together? And I'd let her redecorate to this extent? I didn't even recognize the room, although a closer inspection revealed books I definitely owned on the shelf.

I sat down on the bed and opened my day planner. I thumbed through until I found the last date I'd filled in.

It was the day I'd left. Just as it should be.

I narrowed my eyes at it, flipping ahead to make sure all the other entries were blank. Then I went back to today's entry.

"**Do The Thing. You Know. Hospital. Do it, You COWARD.**"

I heard the apartment door open and close. I muttered, "Hey, me," under my breath out of habit. Then, realizing this version of me would have to have all the answers I needed, I jumped to my feet and moved to the bedroom door. It was still ajar, so I could hear voices echo down the hall.

"Did you go outside?" Blonde asked.

"No, I just got home."

"No, you got home a few minutes ago and then went to get cleaned up. Why'd you go outside?" A pause. "Did you change clothes?"

I heard myself say, "Oh, for crying out loud. Hold on a second."

I stood up just as another me appeared in the doorway. She was wearing a very nice blouse, buttoned all the way to the collar. Her hair was very, very short but stylish, and she was wearing big glasses. They were almost too big for her face, but it kind of worked for us. She glanced over her shoulder and then stepped into the room.

"When are you from?" she whispered, shutting the door behind her.

"Now."

A line appeared between her eyebrows. "You can't be from *now*. I'm from *now*."

"I'm from *today*," I said, pointing at the cover of the day planner. "When the hell are *you* from?"

"I haven't even traveled today," she said, sounding angry now. "I haven't traveled in a year and a half."

I was stunned. I'd never gone that long between trips before. I couldn't even imagine what would make me stop.

"Then what does this mean?"

I held up the day planner again like a smoking gun. It was still open to today's date, so I saw that the page looked different. The entry had changed. I brought it closer and read the new words.

"Meeting with Creatives, Confirm Deadline!"

"Creatives?" I said. "What the hell does that mean?"

"Sweetie?" Blonde said from the hallway.

I looked at the closed door. "Who is that?"

"I thought you were from now," the other me said. "If you were really from now, you'd know your own fiancée. So when are you *really* from?"

I couldn't process the words. I couldn't even begin to understand what she was saying. So I did what I always did when I was cornered, confused, and scared.

I dropped the day planner and got the hell out of there.

CHAPTER TWO

Okay, I should probably explain some of this before we go any further. First, my name is Chloe Cross. Nice to meet you. I'm in my early to mid-thirties - it's kind of hard to be more exact than that, since I don't operate on quite the same calendar as you, but it's around there. I just tell people thirty-three because it's easier. I'm a chef by profession, and I work at a restaurant called Trilogy. One fact you've hopefully already figured out on your own: I'm a time traveler. I don't have a cool eighties car or a vintage blue phone box. I already said that don't know why or how it happens. There was no lab accident, no big origin story. It's just an ability I always had that I learned to control. Somewhat.

I only need to think about going somewhere else and "poof," I'm gone. I can sort of control when I go by concentrating on a certain date. The where is mostly a crapshoot. Let's say I want to go back to Christmas, 1999. I would think about that date, and then I'd show up within a few miles of where I originally was on that Christmas morning. I usually end up in the same city, but there doesn't seem to be a logic to it. Probably something to do with Earth's rotation and, uh, moving through space, orbits, I don't know. A scientist probably could work out the exact parameters, but I always failed those classes in school. I have a general idea, though, and I can work with it.

Being tethered to my past self like that means I can't jump outside my own lifetime. But that's fine. It means I don't have to answer big questions like the 'killing baby Hitler' thing. Even if I did, I've discovered that for the most part, the things I do in the past seldom have any big effect on the present-day. If I did kill baby Hitler, I would come back to find someone had switched babies at the hospital and the same little demon-weasel had done his same horrors and I'd accomplished nothing.

I always laugh at *Back to the Future* because the idea of one sports almanac causing so much chaos was ridiculous. Marty screwed up his parents meeting, but they still ended up getting together at the same time. That's how it works for me. No matter what happens in the past, I can count on recognizing the world when I get back home.

Until now, I guess.

There shouldn't have been a strange woman in my apartment. I had jumped back to the same day I left, and she was *definitely* not acting like we'd only known each other a few hours. And the presence of another me proved something had gone horribly haywire. When I travel, my whole body goes. There shouldn't have been two versions of me in that apartment at that time unless she was from another time period. But that wouldn't explain the changed day planner.

When I popped out of 2024, I hadn't exactly set a destination for myself. I just wanted to be gone. I opened my eyes and discovered I was a few blocks from the place I lived when I was twenty-three. It was as good a place as any to catch my breath, so I got my bearings and started to walk.

I was just around the corner from my old building when I ran into myself walking from the other direction. She was wearing that old peacoat I loved, her hair was short, and she was wearing glasses instead of contacts. She was looking at her phone and glanced up at me when I stepped in her way. She did a double-take and then took a step back.

Oh. That's another thing I should clarify. I don't remember this meeting, even though it happened in my past. It didn't happen until I, current me, went back to do it. Later on, it would exist in my memory like anything else, and I would remember running into an older me on the street on this particular day and anything that we were about to say to each other. But as it was happening, I was as clueless as she was about what would happen next.

"You look like we've been through a lot," Glasses said.

"You could say that. It's been a day."

"What do you need?"

"Just a quiet place to think for a little bit."

Glasses turned off her phone screen and slipped it into her coat pocket. When her hand came out, she was holding her keys. She held them out and dropped them into my hand.

"You're working at Laflin's now, right?" I said.

She nodded. "And I'm running late for my shift. Will you be okay for a few hours?"

"No problem, sure," I said, slipping the keys into my pocket.

"Okay."

She stepped around me and kept walking. I watched her go before I went on my way as well.

When I got to the apartment, I stopped and looked at everything like a detective looking for clues to a murder. Everything seemed to be in the right place. I even recognized the library book on the coffee table. No strangers cooking dinner. No unexplained extra pair of shoes next to the door. I breathed a sigh of relief and let myself relax. It was decorated exactly the way I remembered, and that meant this was a safe place to think.

The apartment was open-space, a single room with a bed against the far wall, a couch acting as the border between public and private space, and a kitchen crammed into one corner. I bypassed the couch and went straight for the bed. I dropped down onto the mattress and sighed. I'd loved this bed. It had been absolutely perfect for my back, and laying on it now was exactly the comfort I needed. Maybe that was why my mind had yanked me here.

I let my feet dangle over the edge of the bed and folded my hands on my stomach. I tried to remember if anything like this had ever happened to me before.

Of course there had never been anything so drastic as a whole new person. But had there been times when I came home and there were tiny differences that I wrote off as a bad memory? And how could I prove it wasn't just forgetfulness if they really were tiny differences? That didn't prove anything. It just proved that I didn't have a photographic memory.

Having an unknown partner was a huge thing. It was a World Breaker. I came up with that when I was a teenager to stop myself from trying anything too drastic in my travels. I was terrified of the butterfly effect. What if I went back in time and did something that made my foster parents get divorced? And then they never took me in, and I got sent to some awful family instead? I told myself I had to be extra careful not to mess anything up.

Eventually, I discovered that it probably wasn't possible to change the future.

So I got lazy.

And now, apparently, I'd broken my world.

Now I had to think about how to get back. If I *could* get back. This wasn't like missing my exit or taking the wrong branch on a hiking trail. I had to figure out what I'd changed and fix it somehow. It seemed obvious that going back to see my mother had to be involved. It was the trip where everything changed. And it *was* a pretty big moment. What if my visit convinced her not to abandon me? That would change everything going forward.

Including now?

I pushed myself up on my elbows and looked around. The apartment definitely looked the same as I remembered. And I had the right job. Would being raised by my birth mother have changed that? God, was I going to have to analyze every single moment of my *entire life* and question the motivation behind every choice? That sounded exhausting. And depressing.

I just wanted to go home. I wanted to sleep in my own bed, my current bed, and go to work, and read my book, and I wanted to pretend I was a normal person whose stupid choices didn't create a whole alternate reality. I didn't feel like that was too much to ask.

Eventually I moved up onto the bed, folded the pillow under my head, and went to sleep. I was exhausted after everything that had happened, and sleep was good. It was healing and comforting and it was the only thing I was entirely sure of at that moment.

I didn't wake up until I heard the front door open. The room had gotten dark while I slept. Glasses turned on a lamp and sat down a bag of takeout from the restaurant.

"Hey," she said. "I wasn't sure if you would still be here when I got home. I brought something anyway, if you're hungry."

"Famished." The smell from the bags was already pulling at me like I was a cartoon dog. I got out of bed and went to join her at the dinner table. I gasped when I saw the bag. "Truelove's! Oh, hell yeah. I haven't had them in forever!"

She frowned. "Why~ oh no."

I winced. "Sorry. Enjoy it while you can."

"Damn." She sighed. "Oh well." She got two plates out of the cabinet and brought them over. "So. Elephant in the room. Do I want to know? Or I guess the question is, should you tell me?"

"I don't know." I honestly had no idea. If I told her not to go back and visit our birthday, would the timeline change so that I ceased to exist? I rubbed my temples. "It's been a rough day. I hit one of those time travel speed bumps that they should write an instruction manual about. I don't think I should do anything drastic until I have more information."

Glasses nodded. She sat down and took one of the to-go boxes for herself. I took the other. "So how long are you planning to stick around?"

Another good question I didn't have an answer for. "Will it be awkward for you if I needed a few days? Just while I'm figuring out my next moves?"

She thought about it for a second. "I'm sort of seeing someone right now," she said finally. "I don't want to say her name because I don't want you to react one way or the other. It's still early."

I tried to remember— oh. Right. Julia. I tried to keep my face neutral, but apparently I failed.

"Oh come on." She dropped her fork and sat up straighter. "Julia?"

I flinched. No point in lying to myself. "Yeah."

"Damn it. I really liked her."

"Sorry."

Glasses sighed. "Do we at least have a good run?"

I mimed zipping my lips.

She shook her head at me. "Well, I guess if it doesn't affect anything, you're free to stay as long as you like." She picked her fork back up. "Damn. That's disappointing. Did she screw up somehow, or was I the problem?"

"No comment."

"This is the *worst*."

I shrugged. "Sorry."

She poked at her food. I had learned a long time ago not to let my future selves affect my current relationships. But it's really to ignore. It's like watching a movie for the first time with someone who has already seen it. A character pops up, you get excited, and then the person next to you says, "Don't get too attached."

"I have a question," I said, hoping to change the subject. "Who were we raised by?"

Glasses looked at me strangely. "What, do you want a list, or...?"

"Foster parents, right?" I said. "Not our mother."

"We never met our mother."

I nodded. "Okay." I looked up at the ceiling. "Okay," I

said again.

She narrowed her eyes at me. "Does this have something to do with our birth mother?"

"No," I said.

"You're lying."

I shrugged, noncommittal. "Some very strange things are going on right now. I can't even say where exactly it started."

"But you can't go home? Back to whenever you're from?"

I started to say no, but that actually wasn't the worst idea. I'd panicked and run away because I was inside my home with a stranger and a version of me that shouldn't have existed. If I went back, I could lay low and play detective. I could research myself and see the differences for myself. The more I thought about it, the more sense it made, and I kicked myself for not thinking of it earlier.

"That might actually be the right step."

"You don't have to sound so surprised. We're pretty clever."

I smiled. "Yeah, we are." I took a few bites of my food - delicious - and stood up. "Thank you. For letting me use your apartment and the food."

"You're welcome." She waved goodbye.

I closed my eyes and left the apartment, sending myself back home. But not "home," to my apartment, just the right time and the right city. Like I said, if I didn't think of a very specific place, I usually arrived wherever the universe decided was convenient. I prayed I didn't end up on the street, seconds away from being run over by a bicycle, or in the middle of a shopping center. Both had happened, and neither was very fun. I'd decided not to waste time being annoyed by that and just be grateful that I'd never popped up in a brick wall or locked in a bank vault.

This time I arrived at an El station. There were two other people waiting, both facing away from me so they didn't see me pop up out of thin air. I walked to a bench and took a seat. Just another commuter. Nothing strange about me at all. Or at least nothing stranger than any other commuter.

The train arrived and the three of us got on. We

dispersed to give each other the appropriate amount of space, avoiding any acknowledgement of each other unless absolutely necessary. True commuters following the unwritten rule of train travel. I sat facing forward and tried to think of how I could do research without my phone. Why hadn't I just slipped my stupid phone into my pocket when I left for the hospital?

An older woman slipped into the seat next to me. I tensed and leaned closer to the window. I tried to make it look casual, normal, not a reaction to Stranger Danger. There were plenty of other seats for her to have chosen, and only a psycho, a homeless person, or—

"Welcome home."

I would have known that voice anywhere. I looked at her for the first time to confirm it. A few extra decades, hair still dark but with too many streaks of silver to ignore. Glasses. She'd lost some weight in the face that did really great things for her cheekbones and jawline. Despite that, my first thought was 'grandmother,' and I felt myself cringe when she gave me a withering look of disapproval.

"You really fucked up that time, kid."

I furrowed my brow. "What?"

"Everything is sorted out now," my older self said. "But it was no small feat. You're lucky you didn't try to go back and fix things yourself. That would've just caused so many more splinters."

I tried to follow her thinking. "Wait. Okay. Wait, are you talking about the woman in my apartment? And that other me—"

"Technically *you* were the other one," the Old Woman corrected. "And don't think of me as 'Old Woman,' of whatever version of it you just came up with. I know how I think and that is *very* route-one thinking. I do not appreciate being saddled with that title."

"Sorry." The problem with interacting with yourself was that sometimes it felt like talking to a psychic. "I-is there something you'd prefer?"

She took a deep breath and sighed, rolling her eyes. "I don't *know*. Chloe?"

"I'm Chloe."

"So egotistical," she said with another sigh. "Fine. Call me the Dame."

I almost laughed, but somehow it fit. "And you call *me* egotistical. So tell me what the hell you're talking about. What did I screw up?"

"You saw for yourself. You changed things enough that a new timeline branched off. Then you jumped and ended up in the wrong one."

"I landed in the wrong timeline?"

She nodded. "Your visit made your mother second-guess her decision to abandon you. You jumped at the exact second she changed your mind. You couldn't have known that, but it really screwed things up. She stayed at the hospital, took you home, raised you until you were ten."

"What happened when I was ten?"

"No idea. One day she jumped and never came home."

I sank back into my seat. So I most likely still ended up in foster care, just later than usual. Those ten years with my birth mother must have changed so much about who I grew up to be. Was it better or worse to have known my mother before losing her?

"You're back where you belong now. You can go home and it will be exactly as you left it. Just try to be more careful next time."

I laughed. "Careful? What does– You just said I couldn't have known I was jumping at the wrong time! What does careful have to do with it?"

She looked at me like I was insane. "You visited our mother. You had a conversation with her moments after we were born. You don't think that might fuck someone up? The difference between growing up in foster care and having a mother for ten years before you go into foster care is huge. That version of your life that you got a glimpse of? It might have seemed pretty close to this one. But trust me, the you in that timeline was a stranger. And you do not want to wind up jumping around the timeline of a stranger."

"I could have ended up jumping in *her* life instead of my own?"

She ignored the question. "You're back on track now. But like I said, be careful. We can't fix your problems every time you get sloppy."

"*We?*"

"We. Us. You and me and the others."

I pressed my lips together and crossed my arms over my chest.

"Oh, don't pout," she said. "I'm not being mean. This is just how you act when you have to interact with yourself as a teenager. Right?"

"So I'm just stupid my whole life?"

"Yes," the Dame said with a smile. "But the good thing is that you're blind to the stupidness while you're inside it. So you might as well have fun while you can."

I grunted. It wasn't much comfort, but it would do for now.

"Go home," she said. "Rest. And don't jump for a while. After all this, you need to reset your anchors and settle."

"You have a point there," I said.

"Of course I do." She looked around to make sure the other passengers were still ignoring us. "Okay. Have a nice life. See you in a few decades."

And then she was gone. There wasn't a sound, a flash of light, or even a noticeable change. The seat next to me was just suddenly empty again. You've probably experienced something similar to that. You're certain you're alone and then you look up, and BOOM! Sudden person out of nowhere. I come and go sort of like that. I kind of just slip in between the moments.

I looked out the window, grateful to know I was home. I'd felt the panic at the back of my skull, tickling, threatening to sprout and infect my whole brain. No home base, nowhere to retreat, no safe place... but it was all settled now. The mystery was basically solved, even if I didn't quite understand what I'd done wrong or how I could avoid it in the past. The version of me that wanted to be called the Dame had fixed things. For that I was grateful.

Even though I'd slept for hours at Glasses' apartment, I couldn't wait to get back to my own bed. I wanted to sleep for twelve hours and wake up in the right place. Reset all the clocks and get back into the proper rhythm.

It had been a weird-ass day. I took comfort in the fact it was almost over, by any metric you wanted to use.

I prayed tomorrow would be a little easier on me.

Chapter Three

Things returned to normal after that. Or at least as normal as it could have been. I don't know your experiences. It seemed normal to me. I went back to 1999 to see a Backstreet Boys concert my foster parents hadn't let me see. It was as awesome as I hoped it would be. But that was the only trip I took. I was a little jumpy about... jumping. I decided to play it safe and just chill out. Mostly I went to work and hung around my apartment. I had almost lost this simple, stupid life that I'd built for myself, and I was determined to stop taking it for granted.

Of course, that very important and mature lesson was all but forgotten by the first weekend after my encounter with the Dame. Yeah, I'd almost lost everything. But then I didn't and everything worked out fine. It's like if you have a near-miss with a bus nearly hitting you walking home from work. You'd be shaken up for a while but eventually you would get over it and move on with your life. It's something humans are extraordinarily good at. And, as far as I know, I am a human.

(And let me pause to clarify I'm not trying to minimize

trauma here. Sometimes people have a near-miss and it screws them up for life, and that's not a failing on their part. I know PTSD is a thing and it can change a person's life. I know that! It's a sloppy metaphor, and I'm rambling, so I'm just saying I'm not good at learning from my mistakes. Let's get back to the story...)

Six weeks or so after I visited my mother, I came home from work to find myself sitting on my couch. She looked to be mid-teens, with an unfortunate spattering of acne just under her left eye. She was swimming in two layers of baggy clothes, her hands and feet swallowed by the material. Her hair was center-parted and tied in braids that hung down over either shoulder.

She looked me up and down in that awful, judgmental way all teenagers possess. I bristled, then realized how idiotic it was to feel judged by myself. Still, teenagers.

"I couldn't figure out your TV," Baby said.

"Welcome to the future." I put down my bag and closed the door. "What are we running away from this time?"

"You don't know?"

I shook my head. "I don't remember running away to the future. At least not this far. It won't lock in until you leave and it becomes part of our history."

"But you already lived this part of your life."

"Yeah," I said, grunting as I dropped myself down onto the couch next to her. "Time travel rules are weird."

She was looking at me with disgust again. "What was that?"

"What?"

"That... *sound* you made when you sat down."

"I didn't..." I realized something horrible. "Don't think of me as Old Woman."

She cringed just enough that I knew I was right. "I wasn't," she lied.

I shook my head. "So? Go on, why are you here? Bad foster family?"

"Nah, they're fine." She pushed up the sleeves of her sweatshirt and fiddled with her fingernails. "I was worried someone might be here when I showed up."

I remembered walking in on my fiancée and nodded. "That happens sometimes. Not right now, unfortunately."

Baby nodded slowly. "Cool. I mean, good. Not good. I'm sorry there's nobody."

"It's fine," I said, chuckling. "Being single isn't the worst thing in the world."

She twisted her lips. "Are we gay?"

"Ahh. You're *that* age." I looked at her again and did some mental math. I smiled knowingly. "Alicia, right?"

She refused to look at me, but her cheeks got red.

I laughed and patted her knee. "Yeah. We're gay. And Alicia... Alicia... what was her last name?"

"Alicia *Scott*." She looked at me accusingly. "How could you forget her?"

"It's been a few years," I said. "And there have been a lot of other 'Alicias' since then."

"Oh god, am I a slut?"

I slapped her knee. "Easy! Not *a lot*. There's a... reasonable amount. Besides, I barely remember anyone I went to high school with. Give me a break. But Alicia was special. I guess she *was* my awakening."

"Do... do we ever... I mean, if I asked her out~"

"Sorry, bud," I said. "But she's straight."

Baby looked crushed.

"Don't worry about it too much. No one gets with their first crush. It's like a universal law. Don't worry. The lesson here is that no matter how much you're obsessed with her now, no matter how much it will hurt when she walks away for the last time, eventually Alicia becomes a footnote on a much more fun journey."

She sighed and sagged back, slumping on the couch. "So... is this real?"

I looked at her. Was I really the sage old traveler who taught myself how this worked? I guessed at that age, being close to forty definitely made me an elder. Still, I felt bad for originally thinking of the Dame as old.

"Yeah. It's real. I'm you in a few years."

She ran her eyes over me again. "That's cool... I guess..."

I gestured at myself. "I think we turned out pretty cool."

She eyed my white chef's jacket with Trilogy stitched on the pocket. "We work at a restaurant."

"Head chef," I said.

"Do you get to wear the hat?"

"Yep."

"Lame." Something about the way she said it made me smile, let me know what she really thought. God forbid she let an adult see she was impressed, even if that adult was herself.

"Do you want to stay for dinner?"

She shook her head. Sighed again. God, did teenagers just have a ton of extra air inside of them? She sat up and scooted to the edge of the couch.

"I should probably go do some homework. Thanks for letting me chill for a while. And answering my question." She stood up and pulled at the drawstrings of her hoodie. "*Nothing* with Alicia? We don't even, like, make out at a party or something?"

I shook my head sadly. "Sorry, kid."

She sighed yet again. Then she lifted her hand in farewell and disappeared from my living room.

I sat in the apartment and thought about the visit. I chewed my bottom lip, then took out my phone and opened Facebook. It was a pretty common name, so I didn't actually expect any real results. I typed in ALICIA SCOTT and hit enter, half ready to close the app as soon as the list of certainly-unrelated accounts loaded.

Instead, the top result was an Alicia Scott who lived in Chicago. And even from the thumbnail, I could tell she was the right age and resembled the one I had crushed so hard on back in high school. I clicked on her profile and scrolled through her unlocked posts. It was just a little harmless snooping. There was nothing wrong with that. It was the whole purpose of social media, to check out people from your past and see where they ended up. Nothing wrong with that. She'd never even know unless I did something stupid.

I opened Messenger. "Hey, stranger! Blast from the past. I'm sure you don't even remember me, but we had fourth period together. The internet can be weird sometimes, right? Just wanted to say hi!"

Yes, that was stupid. But it didn't have to mean anything. People liked to be remembered. She would see the message in a day or two, she might respond with an emoji or something, and then we'd both go on with our lives—

"CHLOE CROSS! OMG!"

I raised an eyebrow at the reply. I moved my hands to type, not sure what I intended to say, but she sent a second message before I could make my brain work.

"You're still in Chicago, too! Amazing! How have we never hung out??"

"Bad luck, I guess?" I sent back. "How have you been?"

"Wayyyyyyyyyy 2 much 2 type it all out here. If we're both in the same city, we HAVE to meet up and get drinks or smthng."

"Absolutely. Do you know Trilogy?"

"Oh wow, that's ELITE. I've only been there once but I've been dying to go back. Can you actually get us in??"

I blushed the way Baby had blushed earlier, and I kind of hated myself for it. I would wait and reveal the truth about working there in person. "I can absolutely get us in for lunch. My treat. I'm free Friday afternoon if that works for you."

"I can move some things around. I can't wait to see you!"

"Same," I typed.

I put my phone down. I had no doubt she was currently going through my social media, seeing what she could learn about me before we were face-to-face again. She wouldn't find much. Social media seemed to be a way for people to chronicle their lives and keep track of their pasts. I didn't need crutches like that. Still, I was excited at the idea of revisiting someone I hadn't seen in so long. I was positive that whatever childish feelings of lust I might've had for her were long dead, so I didn't even have to worry about it feeling like a date.

***

I'm honestly not sure how we ended up sleeping together. It absolutely was not my intention, and I went into our meet-up with only pure expectations. We met at the restaurant and I got to feel like a celebrity when the hostess and waitress both greeted me by name. I came clean when we'd been seated and she said I was smart for using the job to my benefit. So we had a few drinks. She was still pretty, even though she looked completely different than I remembered. In high school, she'd had blonde hair that was always cut short. Now it was long and dyed black, and it got wavy at the ends. She wore black-rimmed glasses that accented her high cheekbones. I considered going back to see if I was picturing teenage-her correctly, but an adult hanging around a high school trying to get a look at a student... that never ended well.

We chatted for a while about mutual friends, but very quickly figured out we didn't have much in common. Not back then, definitely not now. But that was fine. I didn't expect a lifelong friendship to bloom, and it really was nice catching up.

Near the end of the meal, thanks to the drinks, I confessed that she was my first crush. She told me she was extremely flattered, but straight, and she'd never thought of being with another woman, but very flattered, and it was definitely the ego boost she needed, even though she was definitely straight. She had been divorced for two years, though, and she "joked" that if she ever got curious she would give me a call. I told her I'd be waiting by the phone.

I kissed her cheek when we left the restaurant. She laughed nervously and kissed my cheek in return. Then she looked at me, made a 'what the hell' noise, and kissed my lips.

Twenty minutes later, she was on my bed, and I was on my knees helping her toward her first orgasm in over two years. Then her second. Then her third and, after she repaid the favor with me, her fourth. We took our time and made sure each round was good enough to serve as a grand finale. By the end, my jaw was so sore that part of me wanted to wrap a scarf around my head to keep it in place. It had been well worth the soreness, though, just for the sounds Alicia had made.

When we finally declared it game over, we collapsed on opposite ends of the bed. She was resting against the headboard and I was propped up by pillows on the foot of the bed.

"I like that you kept your glasses on," I said.

She grinned and touched the frames. "Well, I needed to take notes so I could follow your lead."

"You're a good student."

"Thanks." She rubbed her foot against my bare hip. "I'm really glad you got in touch. Did you just randomly think of me out of the blue?"

I nodded. "Yeah. I was thinking about the old days, you know. I wonder what would've happened if I had the courage to actually talk to you back then."

"Back then," Alicia said, "I probably would have called you names and then made your life a living hell. Just implying I might be gay or bi would've been enough to make you an enemy." She brought her hands up to tuck her hair behind her ears. "Now, though... When you said you had a crush on me, I was flattered. But then we kept talking and I kept thinking about it. It didn't seem so crazy. And I might as well explore and try to figure things out, right?"

"Right," I said. "I'm happy to be your guinea pig. If you need to run any further tests, you know how to find me."

Alicia laughed and looked around the room. "Is there a clock somewhere?"

I pointed. "If you need to leave, you don't have to make up an excuse. I understand you might need some time alone to think."

"I appreciate that," she said, scooting to the edge of the bed. "But if we're going to be totally honest, I actually do want to stay. Because I feel like as soon as I leave, I won't get the courage to come back here. Not because I regret it or it was bad. I am so glad it happened and it was *so* good..." Her face changed. "For me. Oh God. Please tell me—"

I laughed. "I had a fantastic time. Don't worry about that. No complaints."

She breathed a sigh of relief. "Okay. Good. But yeah, it's not because of any of those things. It's just because coming back would mean... a lot of things that I'm not ready to commit to right now."

"You don't have to explain. I get it."

I sat up and reached for her. She leaned closer and we kissed. She was tentative at first, but eventually took the lead. When the kiss ended, I stroked her hair.

"All kidding and joking aside, now you know something about yourself. And you can do as much or as little as you want with that information."

"Oh, I'll definitely do something with it." She stroked my jawline and laughed gently. "I had no idea this would happen when I got your message."

"Did you even remember me?"

"Oh yeah. I definitely remembered you. You could always make me laugh. And you used to wear those cool T-shirts!" She laughed and covered her mouth. "God, I'm thinking about it now. Sometimes I spent all day trying to guess what you'd be wearing. I'd be a little disappointed if I saw you in the hallway first. Like it was spoiling the surprise." She sighed and searched my face again. "Yeah. You know, who knows. Maybe if you had asked me out back then... maybe a lot of things would've been different."

"Who knows," I said.

"If we could turn back the clock, right?" She sighed wistfully and finally pulled away.

I watched her gathering her clothes, slowly getting herself ready to head back out into the day and her real life. If we could turn back the clock. Go back in time. Change things.

If I went back now, to the moment right after Baby visited, and encouraged her to be brave and make a move... would it change the world before I got back? Maybe if I jumped home before she actually did anything, I could beat whatever ripple effect it caused. At least then there'd be some universe where Alicia Scott and I actually~

"Are you okay?" she asked. She was mostly dressed already, her shirt hanging open. "You have a weird look on your face."

"No, yeah, sorry. Just thinking."

Alicia bent down and kissed me again. "Thank you for a very surprising day."

"Always happy to help."

She let herself out of the apartment. I dropped down onto the mattress and stretched my arms over my head. Maybe a world already existed where I'd dated her in high school. Just like there was a world where I was currently engaged to the mystery woman who cooked me dinner.

It was certainly something worth thinking about.

CHAPTER FOUR

So there are multiple universes. An uncountable number of other versions of the world where everything I do in the past actually *does* make a difference. And given what happened when I accidentally walked in on blondie, there was a chance I could slip over into one of those realities if I... if... maybe the timing...? "The Dame" said that it happened because I jumped at the exact wrong second, but that didn't seem like something I could plan ahead of time. It would be like trying to take a picture of lightning. I spent the next week or so thinking about whether it would be possible. I literally lost sleep thinking about the possibilities and potential way I could make it happen.

I also had to consider whether or not I *wanted* to make it happen again. I liked my life. It wasn't great, but who was to say another life would be any better or worse? Maybe I go back and hook up with Alicia, we fall madly in love, but then she breaks my heart so badly that it takes me years to recover. Depending on how long we were together, that would mean I might never date Sarah, Brad, Marie, or Debra. Actually, I could do without Debra in my history. But the others all had their good qualities.

Then there was the small issue of the "other" me in the alternate universe. Apparently I wouldn't just slide into a new life like Marty McFly. There would be two versions of me in the same era for a prolonged period of time. I didn't know what might happen in those circumstances. I never spent more than a day, maybe two, in a time period where I already existed. I didn't want to test the consequences of lingering.

Eventually, all the thought of multiverses and timelines and alternate versions of myself turned into a headache, and I was already running on a deficit of sleep. So I made myself drop the subject and moved on with my life. I'd gone this long thinking it was impossible to change the present. It was easier to just go along as if nothing had ever happened. A normal week went by and eventually the idea of hopping from one universe to another had almost faded entirely.

Unfortunately there was another version of me that couldn't let it go.

One day after work, I walked into my apartment and found her sitting on my couch.

She was watching TV. I hung up my jacket and put away my things before I walked over and examined her face, hair, clothes. I actually owned the shirt and jeans she was currently wearing, and our haircut was identical.

"You must be from pretty close by," I determined.

"Tomorrow, actually."

I raised my eyebrows. "Seriously? I make a one day jump?" It wasn't unheard of, but it was like getting in your car to drive to the mailbox.

She smiled and turned off the TV. "One day, and one stream."

I frowned. "Stream?"

"I'm you from another version of reality. The one next door, actually." She wiggled her fingers at me. "Hi, neighbor."

I held up my hands and walked away from her. "Oh, no. No, I decided it's not worth the headache to think about that."

She followed me into the kitchen. "And I decided to keep thinking about it. And I came up with a brilliant idea."

"I'm sure I did." I took a beer out of the fridge and looked at her as I popped the cap.

"You're trying to figure out what to call me?" she said.

"I'm thinking Day-Old," I said. "Like bread."

She narrowed her eyes. "Technically that would be *you*. From my point-of-view."

She had a point there. I took a drink of my beer. "Fine. What do you want to be called?"

"Mastermind."

I scoffed and rolled my eyes.

"Wait until you hear what I have to say," she said. "Then scoff. It's a brilliant plan."

I walked to the dinner table. She followed me. We sat across from each other, me leaning back with my beer and her resting her elbows on the table.

"Okay, Neighbor. Talk."

She wet her lips, took a second to think, and then held up her hands as if to frame her thoughts. "Okay. We figured out that the things we do in the past *can* affect the future. But it's not *our* future. It just creates alternate realities that we normally have no access to. Like you talked to our mother, which created a world where you were raised by her until you were ten. And you ended up getting engaged to that blonde lady."

"But it's impossible to know when to jump so you end up in the changed reality."

She smiled. "That's the beauty of it. We don't even try. We come back to our normal, unaffected world. My plan is creating a world without consequences."

"Which means..."

"We rob a bank."

I stared at her. "Are you sure you're just one reality removed from me? Because I don't think one decision would make me *this* batshit crazy."

Neighbor sat up straighter. "No, it makes sense. Look."

She held her hands up again. "We can go back and scout the bank. Check what happens on a certain day, see who is in the bank and what they do at certain times, look for any openings. We can know exactly when to go in without getting caught. Once we have that information, we can go back to the beginning of the day and actually go through with the robbery. Grab as much cash as we can carry and bring it home to the present-day."

I knew I could time travel with things I held. Otherwise I would show up everywhere naked, and if that was the case, I would just stay put in my own time. I'd never tried it with bundles of cash, but I assumed it was the same principle. So theoretically, her plan might work...

"So... since what I do in the past doesn't have an effect on my present-day, I would come home to a world where the bank had never been robbed?"

"Right. And you'd be holding stacks of cash that had never been stolen."

"But if the bank never got robbed in this timeline, then the stolen money would still exist somewhere."

Neighbor's grin widened. "I thought of that, too. We go back twenty, thirty years. The nineties, maybe. The Federal Reserve destroys old bills all the time. We would just have to claim the money was found in an old safe or something. Buried underground in a dead relative's backyard. We just walk up to the bank and exchange it all for new, fresh bills and no one's the wiser."

"Okay, but even if we do this, it only helps one version of us."

"Ah, no. As you can see, I *can* jump into other realities. So whichever one of us jumps back to the present can go to the other reality to share the other version's cut."

I closed my eyes and massaged my temples. "This is all insane. You realize that, right?"

"Any crazier than what we've been doing our whole lives? Up to this point, we've just been treating it like an amusement park ride. Going back, reliving the highlights, having fun. But we haven't changed our lives in any meaningful way because we thought it was impossible. You figured out the loophole we needed when you created the world where we met our mother. That made such a huge impact, and you left so quickly, that you were able to ride the wave into a universe you didn't belong in. You proved that we can change things."

"I think you're from farther away than you said," I decided. "You're from a universe where someone hit me in the head with a brick."

She pressed her lips together and crossed her arms over her chest. "And maybe *this* is a universe where I'm a stubborn, boring idiot who doesn't recognize opportunity when it's staring her in the face."

"It just sounds so complicated. And we don't need money. We're doing okay for ourselves. We have a job we really like. I don't need 'rob a bank' levels of money."

"Everyone needs that level of money if they can get it without consequences. Are you seriously balking at this because it sounds hard? It'll be worth it. We can keep working at Trilogy. But the difference is we don't have to worry about anything else. *Ever.* Rent goes up? Who cares. Break your leg? Hospital bills won't matter."

I had to admit that did sound pretty nice. Just a pile of money I could dip into when a surprise expense popped up. Peace of mind.

"Peace of mind," Neighbor said, as if she'd read my thoughts.

I cleared my throat and leaned forward. "Let's say we actually do this. What exactly *is* the plan?"

"We can worry about knocking out the details later. Right now I just need to know if you're in or not."

"Give me some time to think about it," I finally said. "It's a pretty big thing to do just on a lark. We're talking about robbing a bank. Even with the benefit of time travel and knowing exactly what will happen in the bank on the day, there are variables we'll have no way of knowing. Once we actually *start* robbing the place, all bets will be off. Maybe there will be a silent alarm we don't know about. Maybe there will be a cop at the diner next door who runs out and decides to be a hero."

"We can do dry runs."

"What?"

She said, "When we go back to the same day multiple times, there's only one time-traveling version of us present. Right?"

She was right. I'd gone back to watch myself graduate high school more than five times. Shut up, it was nostalgic. How many times have you pulled out an old yearbook? Same thing. Anyway, no matter how many times I went to that old cafegymatorium, there were only two versions of me there. One on the stage and one hiding in the back with a baseball hat.

"That's because every time we go back, we're resetting the clock. Otherwise, our lives would just be a horrible cluster of us wandering around Chicago. So we can go back once, see how things are normally. Then we can go back again, and we can test the system. Maybe trigger a false alarm somehow to see how people respond. It's like a video game. You can go through the level as many times as you need to, and when you're ready, you can speed-run through the whole thing with your eyes closed."

"I feel like you've been thinking about this a lot more than one day."

Neighbor said, "It's been over a week since you gave up," she said. "Once the light bulb lit up, it was like a snowball picking up speed and growing, and growing. Do I know for sure this will work? Of course not. But the beauty of our ability is that we don't have to get it right the first time. We get do-overs. We get multiple chances to get things right. And when we do, we'll never have to worry about money ever again."

I chewed my lip and looked at the mouth of my beer bottle.

"Look at it this way," she said. "There's a version of you

out there who says yes to a version of me, and they actually do it, and they end up rich. And we end up with nothing, going about our normal boring lives where we have to check our bank account before we pay a big bill. Which version would you rather be?"

When she put it like that...

"I'm not saying yes," I said. "But I'll think about it."

"Sure," Neighbor said. "Take your time, definitely."

I took a drink of my beer. "I'd offer you dinner, but if you're from tomorrow, then you know I don't have anything in the fridge at the moment."

She nodded. "We could order in."

"Are you hungry?"

"Not really. I ate before I left."

"Yeah, I ate at the restaurant."

I ran my finger over the label of my bottle, then raised my eyes to her. She raised an eyebrow at me. The good thing about talking to yourself, especially one who is close in the timeline, is that you can almost read each other's thoughts. You can just look into her - your... my - eyes and know what's going on behind them. More importantly, you can know if the thoughts in that version of your brain is the same as what's going on in your version. No conversation or awkward questions required.

She stood up first, and I finished my beer before I followed her. By the time I got to the bathroom, she had already started the shower and was undressing in front of the curtain.

I suppose now is the right time to address the fact sometimes I have sex with myself.

I won't go so far as to say I think everyone would do it, given the opportunity. Personally, I think it's stranger - not to mention sadder - if you claim you wouldn't. If *you* wouldn't have sex with you, why in the world would you ever expect someone else to? I bought the subject up with an ex once, and she said that it would be too much like having sex with your twin. But it's nothing like that. Your twin is a completely separate person, even if they have the same features. Having sex with another version of myself is just masturbation with a time delay and an extra pair of hands.

So I got undressed and joined Neighbor in the shower.

At first we just washed each other. Shared the soap and the loofah, washed each other's hair, but then I took her by the shoulders and guided her against the wall. She kissed me, I kissed her back, and I let my hands roam over her body. Her nipples responded to my touch and she made a soft sound as she arched her back. I pulled at her bottom lip when the kiss ended, moving my lips to her neck as my hands moved lower. I stroked her stomach, and she moved her feet apart in anticipation of where I was going next.

Neighbor kissed my hair just before I knelt down in front of her. She hooked one leg over my shoulder and put her hand out to brace herself on the soap rack, putting the other in my hair. That was another perk to having sex with myself; I knew how to make it work with two people in the shower. It required a lot of teamwork and gymnastics.

One of the biggest perks of having sex with yourself - knowing exactly what you like - is also one of the biggest downsides. It's like playing video games with a cheat code. If you don't pace yourself and take care, you end up at the end way too early. That said, this sort of thing isn't about romance. I got her where she needed without teasing or drawing it out any more than necessary. I appreciated lovers who didn't waste my time.

When she stopped trembling, I stood up and pressed her body against the wall with mine. I kissed her, letting her taste herself on my tongue. Her hand made its way between my legs and I turned my hips to give he a better angle to work with. I broke the kiss and put one arm around her shoulders, resting my other hand on her breast. She put her free hand in the small of my back with her fingers splayed.

Neighbor opened her eyes and looked at me.

"Do you really think we can pull this off?" I asked.

She smiled and raised an eyebrow. "We seem to be doing

a pretty good job so far."

I laughed breathlessly. "You know what I mean."

She kissed me and let it linger, pushing me to the edge of orgasm before she pulled back and answered my question.

"I think we're the only people in the world who can actually do this."

I grinned, then I closed my eyes and kissed her as I came.

My whole life had been about impossible things. Talking to my mother moments after my birth, revisiting favorite memories like popping in a home movie, fucking myself in the shower... why not try one more? Why not try the one that could actually change my life for the better?

I pulled back from the kiss. "Let's do it."

"Yeah?" She grinned. "You're in?"

"I'm in." I pressed harder against her. "Let's rob a fucking bank."

Chapter Five

Before we did any actual legwork, we had to choose a bank. It wasn't as easy as I thought it might be, since we would be targeting a location in the past. Because part of Neighbor's plan involved turning in old money that we had "discovered", we had to be sure we went back far enough that the Federal Reserve agreed that the bills were old enough to be destroyed. My first discovery was that all US currency had a lifespan. Singles, fives, and tens were destroyed after about four years. Twenties hung around for five years, and a Ben Franklin was good for close to a decade. But Neighbor wanted to go back farther.

"We're not going back ten measly years," she said. "There's no reason to make things harder on ourselves than they absolutely have to be."

She'd come back to my timeline the day after our first meeting. We were sitting at my dinner table after I got home from work. I'd brought home Chinese for two, since she'd promised to come back to discuss the finer details of our plan. I was still in my uniform, and she was in a black T-shirt and jeans that made our ass look amazing. I had asked her to let me know exactly what pair they were so I could set them aside for special occasions.

"What do you mean harder?"

"We can go all the way back to the late eighties," she said. "There will still be cameras, but connected to VCRs instead of computers or digital archives."

"I suppose that's true." I speared a piece of broccoli. "How can you jump into this timeline?"

Neighbor looked surprised by the question. "It's really not that hard."

"Then show me how to do it."

"You've already done it."

"By accident," I said. "The older version of me said I had to jump at the exact right second. She made it sound impossible, like–"

"Like taking a photo of lightning."

"Right," I said. "Part of this plan involves going back and forth between timelines, and you've shown me that it can be done as easily as time traveling comes to me. I just think it's a skill I should get good at before we actually dive into the plan."

Neighbor dabbed at her lips with a napkin and leaned back. "Technically, you don't have to do it at all. You just have to go back the way you normally do and then come home. Just doing that will be enough to create the other timelines. And since I'm already practiced, it makes sense that I'd be the go-between for everything."

"Do you not trust me?"

"Do you not trust *me?*" Neighbor laughed and shook her head. "You realize how crazy that sounds, right? We're the closest versions of ourselves we've ever met. You basically *are* the person you met yesterday."

"So there's no reason for you not to teach me how to do the thing."

Neighbor said, "There's no reason for you to know how to do it. You've got enough on your plate. You'll be busy enough getting all the details we'll need to actually pull the job. You'll be *creating* the timelines," she said again, poking the table on each word she stressed. "Why would you also need to visit them?"

I didn't really have an answer for that. And since she was right about the fact we were extremely close to being the exact same person, I decided to be honest.

"I just want to know so I can do it myself. I want to see some of the other timelines."

"They're not that interesting."

I raised an eyebrow. "You've been to others?"

She shrugged. "You think you're the first one I visited? First I wanted someone as different from me as possible, mainly just for the variety. So I went as far as possible."

"What did you find?"

Neighbor wrinkled her nose and shook her head. "It was... not pretty. Do you remember in middle school when you took that shortcut home and ran into those stoners by the train tracks?"

"Yeah. That was the first time I thought I was going to get beaten up."

"Apparently there's a version of us who decided to play it cool and pretended she was also into drugs. She stuck around and got high with them to prove she wasn't a narc. Then she started spending more time with them, kept getting high, things escalated from there... The version of me that I visited was a junkie. Multiple failed rehabs, no job, no future."

I was shocked. "That couldn't have been because I smoked pot in middle school. I started smoking it a few years later anyway."

She said, "We started smoking it with Kimberly, in her bedroom. It wasn't the pot, it was the people who came with the pot. They were bad kids to begin with, the drugs were just a... hobby, I guess. So you probably don't have to throw out those joints you have in your sock drawer."

I smiled and finally popped the broccoli into my mouth. I decided to let her think the story had gotten us off the topic of teaching me to jump timelines. I still wanted her to teach me, and I was curious as hell why she was being so cagey about it, but I didn't want to get into an argument with her this early in our partnership.

"Okay. So we're looking at early nineties."

"The earlier the better," she said. "It would be best if the contemporary Chloe Cross looks nothing like us, just in case a witness is able to describe us to a sketch artist. Plus if they get fingerprints and the results lead to a baby, odds are pretty good that they'll think there was a mistake with the records or something."

"That makes sense. I like the nineties. Right before everything went nuts."

Neighbor said, "Definitely seems a lot simpler now, huh?"

I picked up my can of soda and held it out to her. "Here's to simpler times."

She tapped her can against the side of mine. "And here's to being the only person lucky enough to actually go back and appreciate it."

We drank.

The apartment door opened, making us both jump. We were on our feet by the time the door slammed behind the Dame.

"What the hell do you two idiots think you're doing?"

I stumbled over any attempts at speech. Neighbor held up her hands. "Take it easy."

"No!" The Dame jabbed a finger at her. "You don't talk. You're the reason everything is going to hell right now."

"What's going on?" I asked.

The Dame looked between us, then settled on me. "This is your timeline, right? Your home?"

"Right."

"So she..." She jabbed a finger at Neighbor again. "She's the one I'm going to kill."

I stepped between them. "You don't mean literally, right? Because... well, you know the obvious flaw in that plan."

"Technically we're in different timelines." She was still

staring daggers at Neighbor over my shoulder. "So I can kill her without worrying about the consequences to me."

"Well, isn't that lucky," I said. "But maybe we should try talking first."

The Dame took a deep breath and let it out slowly. Then she put her fists on her hips and started pacing. I could tell the desire for violence had gone out of her, but the anger was as strong as ever.

"Let's start from the beginning."

"She showed up here and told you about jumping timelines, right?" The Dame said. "And she had this big plan for how you could use it to rob a bank."

"Right."

"And it seemed like she'd had a lot of time to think it through, right? To work out all the kinks?"

I looked at Neighbor, who was currently staring at her shoes. She was idly stroking her temple with two fingers. It was my tell when I knew I was about to get caught in a lie.

"When did she claim the timelines split between you and her?"

"After you visited me on the train and told me I'd fucked up. She said she kept thinking about the possibilities longer than I had."

"Oh, she was right about that. She kept thinking about it for twenty years. The conversation she had with her older self was *much* different than the one *we* had. Her version of me put this idea in her head. Told her how to get back and forth into this timeline to pull off the plan. She was never going to teach you the trick because she doesn't know how."

Neighbor held out her hands. "Okay! Fine. I lied. But the facts about the plan itself are still the same. It still holds up."

"You have *no idea* what this kind of manipulation can do to reality as a whole. Yes, new branches are happening all the time. Every decision you make creates a new branch. It's like a river that has tributaries going out in all directions. But those happen naturally. What you're planning to do is like sticking a bunch of dynamite in a dam and blowing it up. We don't know what will happen because no one has ever been dumb enough to try it before. But we know it will be bad. That's why we try to stop it."

"Who is 'we'?" Neighbor asked.

"The older version of ourselves," the Dame said. "By the time you're our age, you've figured out a few more tricks about how all this works. You get *smart*. Well, smart-*er*. We keep in touch to make sure there are no slip-ups, like what happened after visiting our birth. Usually, something small like that, we can nudge things back into place. Everything goes on like normal. No harm, no foul. But this bank robbing thing? If any part of it goes wrong, we're talking disaster."

I shrugged. "Okay. So we won't do it."

The Dame shook her head and went into the kitchen. "Not that simple, cupcake." She took a beer out of the fridge and opened it as she walked back to us. "The idea is out there now. She came up with it, and she toddled over here to tell you. She gave you the snowball analogy. Well, it's true. The boulder is already rolling down the hill. Even if you decide not to go through with it, some version of you will, and I have no idea where to find that timeline so I can stop it in time."

"Yeah, she said that part, too," I admitted. "So what do we do?"

She took a long drink from the bottle, draining almost half of it before she finally answered.

"I'm going to help you two idiots rob a fucking bank."

Neighbor looked at me, smirking. "Hey, that's pretty much what you said."

I rolled my eyes.

***

So now we were a trio. Sitting with the Dame at the dinner table felt like we were being scolded by a teacher. A hot teacher. Don't judge me. I already admitted I have sex with myself from time to time, you shouldn't be surprised that I find myself attractive. And I very rarely get visits from versions of myself who are over fifty. It's good for the ego.

I'm getting off track. Neighbor and I went over the plan

we'd figured out amongst ourselves. The Dame listened without interrupting. She kept her hands folded in front of her on the table, thumbs extended with the tips touching. Every now and then she would close her eyes and take a deep breath, and I knew she was holding back on commenting until we were finished. I was getting more anxious with every second. I had already been borderline, despite agreeing. Now that there was a voice of reason in the room, I was doubting the entire undertaking.

When we finished, the Dame placed her hands flat on the table. She directed her critique to Neighbor. "You've skipped a very obvious step."

"What step?"

"You detailed how we'd do recon, figure out the patterns of the morning, where we would take the money, how we would change it for clean, modern bills, and then distribute that to other versions of ourselves."

Neighbor nodded. "Right."

The Dame looked at me. There was desperation in her eyes. A 'please tell me you're not as dumb as she is' fear.

I cleared my throat. "You... We never actually talked about how we'd get the money out of the bank."

The Dame snapped her fingers, knocked the table, and pointed at Neighbor. "Bingo. You haven't come up with the actual bank robbing part of your bank robbery plan."

Neighbor opened her mouth. Closed it. "I-I just figured that would be simple. We go into the vault and pop out to a different time."

"What if you arrive and you're still inside the vault?"

"Why would we still be inside the vault?" I asked. "We almost never arrive in the same place we left from."

The Dame said, "Are you willing to take that risk in a situation with armed guards? No. You have to actually, physically leave the bank with the money before you even think of jumping away. And that is going to be next to impossible."

Neighbor said, "She's going to memorize everyone's

movements. She basically *will* be invisible because she'll know when people are looking in her direction. She can slip past them."

"You think we'll figure out every bank employee's route so well that we can just walk into the vault, fill a bag with money, and walk out again?"

The Dame looked at me. "How many trips do you think it would take to memorize the pattern? To remember when everyone is looking in another direction?"

"It depends on how many people are in the room," I said, already very aware that she had a point.

"It would take too many trips," the Dame said. Then, as firmly as if it had already been decided, she said, "You're going to need a gun."

"No!" Neighbor and I said together.

I said, "I don't think I'm comfortable with the idea of using a weapon."

The Dame said, "That's really the only way you can rob a bank, sweetheart. You can slide a note to the teller, you can make everyone lie face down on the floor while you empty out the till, but none of it works without a weapon."

Neighbor held up a finger. "You said it would take too many trips. That's crazy. We can take as many trips as we want."

"Wrong." The Dame pointed at me. "*She* can go three times, no more. The first time, she sees the patterns. The second time, she confirms the pattern stays the same and she remembers it. Then, the third and final time, is when she gets the money. Each one of those trips will create a new branch. Three is manageable."

Neighbor said, "But four would be a disaster?"

"It's not just the robbery we have to think about. It's this entire situation. Every step of it creates new branches, new timelines, different possibilities. Timelines where you succeed, others where you fail, where you get lucky, where you have setbacks but you manage to overcome it, where one of you betrays the other and vice versa. When I say three is the limit, consider it written in stone. I know a lot more about ourselves and our ability than you do."

I blew out air. "This is a lot of pressure."

"Too late to quit now," the Dame interrupted. "Sorry, kid. But that's just how it is. We're the ones who have to follow the thread. Them's the breaks. The bright side is that we have time to work out the kinks in our plan before we actually do anything. But we have to do it soon. Because you..." She pointed at Neighbor. "You're not going home until this is all over with."

Neighbor tensed. "Sorry, what?"

"You've been crashing back and forth too much. We need to give the barriers a little time to recover. So for the time being, you're stuck here."

"You... the other you... didn't mention anything about that."

The Dame snorted. "Yeah, I bet there's a lot she didn't mention. She should never have given you this crackpot idea to begin with. But that's not your concern. You figure out the bank. I'll figure out how to keep all of this from crashing down around your ears." She stood up and looked down at us. "Have you two already slept together?"

I looked at Neighbor, then shrugged.

The Dame grinned. "I don't blame you. Enjoy it while you've got it."

"You haven't lost it, as far as I can tell," I said.

Her grin widened and she patted my shoulder. "Another time. Get to work, ladies. Time is of the essence."

She walked past me and, when I turned to look, she had already vanished to whatever year she'd come from. I looked at Neighbor.

"I guess you're staying here, then."

"Sounds like it."

The Dame hadn't finished her beer. I reached out and snagged the bottle, drinking the last bit of it. I decided to drop all my anxieties, all my worries, all my uncertainties, and go all in. If I had to rob a bank, and it looked like Neighbor and the Dame had locked me into that path, I was damn sure going to do it right.

Chapter Six

I spent the next day focusing on work, trying not to think about how weird my life had gotten. Not being scolded by a fifty-year-old version of myself or having my clone as a housemate, that wasn't *too* weird. I was used to that level of weird. Sharing a bed with Neighbor would take some getting used to, I admit. Sex with myself was never about romance, so there was never a reason for any version of me to spend the night. She borrowed one of my T-shirts to sleep in, although technically it was *her* shirt as much as it was mine. We tossed and turned for a while and, between us, we probably ended up getting a total of three hours of bad sleep.

After breakfast, when I started getting ready for work, she followed me into the bedroom and stood in the doorway with her arms crossed over her chest. She watched me get dressed, which felt weirder than it had any right to be.

"What am I supposed to do today?"

"Plan the heist," I said. "You heard the Dame. We only get three chances at this. I want to know as much as possible before I even go back. Use the internet to figure out what bank we're going to target. That's job one."

She said, "Sounds like homework."

"This whole thing is your idea. Now you're complaining it's too much work?"

"I thought it would be fun! And excitement! Rolling into the bank with our masks, getting rich, coming back here and fucking on a big pile of cash."

I had to admit, her version sounded fun. "Well, since I'm the one who is risking my ass by actually putting myself in harm's way, I want to know as much as possible."

"Sure, sure," she said.

I finished getting ready. She followed me to the front door. It was like owning a puppy. Even worse, it felt like a one-night stand who was refusing to leave. It didn't matter if it was literally me, I felt a twinge of anxiety leaving her alone in my apartment.

"Try not to make a mess of the place while I'm gone."

"It's my place to mess up."

"No, your place is in that *other* timeline. And if I ever end up there, I'll respect the fact that I'm on your turf."

She waved me off, but I could see she accepted my point. Feeling only slightly better about my apartment's chances of surviving the day, I turned my back on her and put all the bank robbery shenanigans out of my mind.

Despite my time traveling hobby, I really did have a normal life. I was the head chef at a very trendy, very popular restaurant. We were right at the line where eating there counted as a special occasion, but we still served actual food instead of 'combined ingredient experiences.' You might pay a lot for the privilege of dining with us, but you damn well got your money's worth. Thick and juicy steaks, fish as fresh as you could hope for in Illinois, and a vegetarian menu so mouthwatering it could entice the most hardcore carnivore to experiment a little.

None of my coworkers knew about my ability. I never saw any reason to let them in on my secret. The more people who knew, the more chance something could slip. I had been examined by doctors for normal health stuff, and none of them ever saw anything that made them say, 'huh, that's weird, are you unstuck in time...?' so I figure it's not something science could figure out even if I let the cat out of the bag. There was nothing to be gained from it.

Besides, keeping it secret meant that when I was at work, I could feel like a normal person. My coworkers thought I was boring. They had an image of me as someone who sat around my apartment all the time, watching movies and reading books. As far as they knew, I never traveled and rarely dated. It wasn't that far off from the truth. That's who I was a lot of the time, save the occasional trip to watch the Cubbies win the World Series or see Prince in concert.

Just thinking about it was enough to give me the itch. I spent my shift thinking about trips I could take that wouldn't make the Dame angry. Nothing related to bank robbing, of course. Just a little afternoon jaunt to another time to get my mind off what we were planning to do. I cooked on autopilot. I'd made every dish on our menu so many times that I could've done it in my sleep. I thought about visiting myself as a child, or maybe right after I graduated from high school. Or maybe go see *The Sixth Sense* in a theater on opening weekend with a bunch of people who had no idea the twist was coming.

Before, I could always ignore the urge to Do Something Important with my ability because I always said it didn't matter. I couldn't kill Baby Hitler because I was born too late, but I also couldn't... I don't know, warn people about 9/11 because the timeline was always the same by the time I got back. I figured any attempt to change the course of history would be a waste of energy. But now I knew that if I succeeded, it *would* have an effect on other realities.

Then again, if there really were other realities, there would already be versions of the world where 9/11 didn't happen. So I didn't need to try making another one.

My sous chef, Erin, brushed by me and checked my salmon. "You look like you're a thousand miles away," she said. "What are you thinking about?"

"If you went back in time, would you go see *Sixth Sense* or try to stop 9/11?"

She blinked at me. "Are those really my only two options?"

"No."

She tilted her head to the side and looked up at the ceiling. After a few seconds, she said, "Invest in Google. Or Amazon. One of those."

"I can't fault you on that one."

"How about you?" she said. "Where would you go?"

"That's what I'm trying to figure out. So many options, you know? Hard to decide."

Erin nodded and turned her head in response to a waiter calling from the pass-through. She pointed at my fish. "You're burning."

"Shit."

By the time I'd corrected my near-mistake, Erin was gone. It wasn't a bad idea, investing in the eventual corporate overlords no one saw coming. It would be a much easier way to get another version of myself rich. Then, Neighbor and I could just hop over to that timeline and rob ourselves instead of robbing a bank. I twisted my lips and raised an eyebrow. I had intended it as a joke, but the more I thought of it, the more I liked the idea. Why couldn't I just make a version of myself rich and target her? It made so much sense and was a much smaller risk.

I figured out what the Dame would say before my shift ended. *There's a version of this where you do that instead.* I could almost hear the weary sigh in her voice. *That timeline existed before you even thought of the idea. The bank robbery idea exists here and now, and we're the ones involved with it. We're the ones who have to pull it off.*

I wish I knew how and why she was so certain. I would find out eventually, since I would become her in twenty years, but I wanted to know now. I wanted to understand. God, how many times had I told a past version of myself that knowledge would come in time, answers would be there when I needed them, everything happens when it's supposed to? I was the queen of 'don't skip to the end of a book to find out how it all ends' and 'the journey is more important than the destination.'

But damn it, I wanted to *know*. I'd wondered about this my entire life. How I could time travel, why I was apparently the only one who could do it. And this older version of me had apparently not only figured it all out, she'd taken it upon herself to police the younger versions of us that tried to mess things up. I wanted to know how and when I became that person. I wanted to be her more than anything.

After work, I left the restaurant and walked to the El station. Halfway there, I closed my eyes and focused on a random day. It didn't matter when, so I focused on summer. Mid-afternoon. When I opened my eyes, I was still on the same street but different. The setting sun had reversed several degrees across the sky and changed the angle of all the shadows. I could smell coffee from the shop on the corner. A cluster of students were at the corner, waiting on the light to change.

It was kind of nice not knowing when I was. Nowhere to be, any responsibilities I might have already being undertaken by the contemporary me. I could hop on the bus downtown and spend the afternoon wandering a museum before I went back to deal with Neighbor.

I joined the students at the light. The next time I saw Erin, I would tell her I'd figured out the answer to my question.

If you could go back in time, the perfect destination was a random afternoon on a nice day where you didn't have anything to do or anywhere to be.

I smiled to myself as I crossed the street and, for the first time since Neighbor showed up, I felt like I could breathe.

"Chloe...?"

Shit. I almost stopped walking in the middle of the street, but I kept moving until I was safely on the sidewalk. Only then did I turn around to confirm one of my worst nightmares was coming true. Nina Ferguson was hurrying to catch up with me. I regretted that I hadn't checked the date. My reaction to seeing her really depended on when this was. She was smiling, definitely happy to see me, if a little confused. I decided to follow her lead.

"Oh hi!" I said. "Funny running into you here."

Her happy-confused ratio tipped farther to the latter. "My shop is right around the block. Were you coming to see me?"

"No," I said a little too quickly. "Uh, I mean, no, I wasn't really going... anywhere in particular. I was just walking."

"Are you on break?"

"Break?" I realized I was still in my work clothes. "Yeah. Uh, yeah, I was just..." I hooked my thumb over my shoulder. "Getting a little air. Stretching my legs. Getting my steps in." I forced a laugh.

Nina nodded slowly, cautiously. "Okay. Well. Great, um. Do you have time to come hang out for a bit? Get a coffee?"

"Shoot, I really don't. Sorry..."

"Don't be. I'm just glad I saw you. Are you sure everything's okay?"

I nodded. "Yeah. No, I just..." I gestured again. "I-I have a thing to get back to."

"Right." Nina narrowed her eyes. "Well. Okay. I'll talk to you tonight."

"Fantastic."

I waved goodbye, then turned and walked away as fast as I could without running. Of all the streets, and all the days in all the years, I had to run into *her*. It's bad enough running into your ex without warning. It's a whole other beast to run into them with no idea where you are in the relationship. This was apparently still during the good part, which meant I had to pretend I didn't know she was secretly a paranoid lunatic who would eventually cheat on me with some dude she worked with. She even tried to blame me for cheating, saying I cheated on *her* first. She even claimed she caught me once when~

I stopped walking.

When I was supposed to be at work, but I was downtown by her shop acting weird.

I turned and looked back the way I'd come. Nina was already gone. Apparently this moment in time was one of those events where I actually *did* affect my own life with time travel. I knew I couldn't blame our entire breakup on this one odd interaction, and she had definitely made the choice to sleep with someone else all on her own, but it was surreal to see the other side of the situation. Sure, I was acting strange. But if she'd just asked me what was going on, current-me would have figured out who she actually met. She would've come up with a lie that smoothed things over.

I started walking again and slipped back to my rightful time. There was no chance I'd be able to relax after that run-in, and knowing what it had led to. I hated not knowing the rules of jumping. I hated that sometimes there were no consequences and sometimes there were huge epic life-changing consequences. I hated that I only had the Dame's word that the bank robbery would be one of the former and not the latter.

I didn't even care about the money anymore. The sooner we were done with this bank shit, the better.

Chapter Seven

First National Bank stood on Michigan Avenue facing the river. Or at least it did in 1990. I walked across what was still called the Michigan Avenue Bridge, still twenty years from being renamed DuSable, and stopped next to one of the ornately carved bridgehouses. I needed to take a second to process what I was about to do. This was still the first trip, but it was important that I treat it like the real thing. I needed to see everything, I needed to get every detail right, and I only had two chances before the Big Event.

The street around the building was free from cops, which was a good sign. I had been half afraid the day we'd chosen - a random day in July, nothing significant recorded anywhere online - would turn out to have a CPD parade taking place directly in front of the bank at the moment of truth. But we were lucky, and the timing had been perfect. It was just after ten in the morning. Too early for the lunch rush, too late for people on the way to work. Probably one of the slowest times of the day.

The target itself looked like any generic bank. Tall

columns, dark glass, seamlessly blending into the downtown architecture of Chicago. I crossed the street with my hands in my pockets, checking to make sure no one was following me. The Dame had tried to convince me there was no reason to be nervous. It was the ultimate crime of convenience. No one would be suspicious of me because I hadn't been seen casing the bank. I'd never been there in my life. I was just like anyone else walking through the doors for the first time.

I didn't even have to wear a disguise because, when I came back for the second trip, this moment would be erased. No VHS tapes of my face. No one recognizing me from another morning. A complete and total do-over. So no reason for subterfuge. But it felt strange taking off my sunglasses and pushing my hair out of my face like I didn't have a care in the world.

Inside, the bank lobby was surprisingly vast. Black and white floor tiles, faux marble walls, a bank of tellers conducting their business behind plexiglass. I had been to the past enough that I wasn't thrown by the lack of computers, but it never looked normal to me. There were pneumatic tubes on the wall like glass columns and, every few seconds, little plastic bullets shot through them going toward god-knew-where.

I counted the tellers - four men, one woman - and the customers - three men. Two of the glass-fronted offices to my right had men in suits talking on their phones, while the other five offices seemed empty. I meandered toward a tall desk in the center of the space, near a bank of plastic plants and chairs for customers to wait for a bank employee to help them. I examined the deposit slips and toyed with the chain tethering the pen to the desktop.

"Can I help you, ma'am?"

I spun around, startled by the sudden appearance of the security guard. In a situation like this, I was hoping any security guards would be retired. Old and gray. This guy was about my age, maybe a little older, with a touch of silver at his temples. He had been sitting in a chair next to the entrance, in the blind spot of anyone coming inside. Crafty bastard. He didn't seem to be carrying a gun, despite his police-like uniform, but I had no doubt he could make my life particularly miserable if I didn't nail the story the Dame had given me.

"I'm waiting for my friend. She's loaning me two hundred dollars and she needs to withdraw the cash." I smiled as sweetly as I could muster. "She was supposed to be here already. She must be running late."

He relaxed slightly. "Let me know if you need anything."

"Absolutely I will. Thank you!"

He nodded and returned to his hidey-hole. He would be a problem, but that was the point of this scouting mission. Now I knew he was there. I could plan for him. I hoped I wouldn't have to hurt him. That was the worst part of this entire situation. If I had to hurt anyone, even slightly, I didn't think any amount of cash reward would be worth it.

I went to one of the padded chairs in front of an empty office and sat down. I could see most of the lobby from this vantage point, and it would be reasonable for me to be bored enough to turn my head so I could see the rest. Just a lady waiting for her friend. Nothing suspicious. I was wearing a gray skirt and a button-down white shirt under a red sweater. I felt the outfit might say the fab 60s than the hip 90s, but I wanted people to think 'Laurie Petrie' when they looked at me. Innocent. Naïve. In no way dangerous or worth worrying about.

I tapped my foot on the tile and folded my hands in my lap. One more benefit to coming back this far for the plan: no cell phones. My claim about meeting up with a friend didn't require an added explanation for why she couldn't call about a change of plans or text to reschedule. I could sit there and wait for up to half an hour before I reasonably gave up on her. Hopefully half an hour would be long enough to get the information we needed.

I kept track of everyone who came in the doors. Construction worker. People in suits. Women in gorgeous clothes that I probably couldn't have afforded even in 1990 dollars. No police, either inside or that I saw passing by on the street. I kept my eyes moving.

The security guard settled into the chair next to me, and I gasped. My surprise had been real, but I played it up like I was in a cartoon. "Lord, you move like a mouse!"

He laughed and tapped his badge. "Trick of the trade. It helps."

"I'm sure it does." I turned my attention back to the door.

"I'm starting to worry you've been stood up."

I smiled and tilted my head to the side. "You don't know Rita. She's *always* stuck in traffic or losing her watch. Lord knows how many times I've finished a whole entrée waiting for her to show up at the restaurant."

He laughed softly. "Well, friend or... whatever... I think it's a crime for *anyone* to leave a woman like you waiting."

I turned to look at him. I realized he was flirting. "Oh! Well, aren't you sweet."

He cleared his throat and shifted in his seat. "If I'm not being too forward... I would love to take you out some night. If you're free, that is."

Shit. "Oh, that's very flattering, but I'm afraid I'm engaged."

His smile didn't even flicker. He shrugged, a player who had been denied a game, and pushed himself up. "I would've kicked myself forever if I didn't at least try. He's a lucky fella."

"I'll make sure he knows it!"

He laughed, touched his brow, and ambled back to where he'd been sitting. I let my smile wither and brushed my hand across my face to disguise it.

It wasn't that he'd asked me out. It was that he had *noticed* me. Which meant that even if my next visit was a complete redo, he would be the same man, and he would notice me again. And he would absolutely be able to give a good description to the police on the third attempt, when I showed up to do the actual robbery. The Dame seemed sure that it wouldn't matter if they knew what I looked like, but I still didn't want my description floating around in connection to an unsolved crime in any timeline. I would have to wear some kind of disguise to keep him from paying any attention to me.

I spent forty minutes inside the bank, which I figured was a good enough chunk of time. If I wasn't in and out in that time frame, something would have to have gone terribly wrong. Luckily I had the best escape plan ever: I would just skip out to a different time. And since I was always tethered to my physical location, I would choose a day when I wasn't in Chicago to ensure I didn't arrive inside the bank. Easy-peasy.

I nodded goodbye to the security guard when I left. He gave me a bashful smile, and I was happy he wouldn't remember our awkward encounter.

"I hope everything works out," he said.

"Fingers crossed. I should've known better than to trust Rita would actually be here." I sighed heavily, rolled my eyes, and shrugged. "I'll find another way, don't worry."

"Good luck."

"Thanks so much."

I waited until I was out of sight from the bank to skip back to the present. I breathed in the air of 2024 and smoothed my hands down the front of my clothes before I started walking.

When I got back to my apartment, Neighbor and the Dame both got to their feet in anticipation. I held up a finger to stop them before either one could talk. I opened my laptop, sat down, and started typing as soon as I could open a word processor. Neighbor came up behind me to read what I was typing, while the Dame crossed her arms and waited patiently.

"They weren't too busy, it looks like," Neighbor said, reading the report. "No police, but a security guard hidden by the door who noticed me."

"Noticed how?" the Dame asked.

I didn't stop typing. "He asked me out."

The Dame grunted and shook her head. "That might be a problem."

"I know. I'll dress down for the next trip."

Neighbor looked me up and down. "Less than this...?"

"Hey! These are your clothes, too. Besides, on the actual robbery jump, I'll be as bland as I can manage. It'll be fine."

"Okay. You've actually been there. You've seen what the bank looks like during the window you're aiming for." The Dame looked skeptical but she didn't argue. "Do you think it's possible?"

I took a breath and considered the question before answering. The lobby would look exactly the way it looked today. The same amount of people, doing the same things. Even without the second trip, I was confident that I had a good grasp of what would happen and what to expect. The guard was really the only red flag, and I felt like I could dissuade him from taking an interest.

"I think so," I said.

"Then I'll take your word for it. When do you want to do the second trip?"

I shrugged. "No time like now."

The Dame shook her head. "Everything is too fresh in your mind right now. You need to let it settle first. That will help you notice details you missed the first time around. You don't watch a movie and then immediately watch it again. We'll wait until at least tomorrow. You did a good job today."

"Thanks." She started to turn away, and I stopped her by holding up my hand. "Actually, I do have one question. It's not important, it's just been bugging me."

The Dame faced me again and raised her eyebrows in invitation.

"What do you two call me?"

They looked at each other. "What do you mean?" Neighbor said.

"Well, you're Neighbor and you're the Dame. But I think of myself as Chloe, because I'm me. But I imagine you both think of yourselves as Chloe because... well." I waved it off. "Neither of you have said what name you've given me. It doesn't matter. I'm just curious."

"Robber," the Dame said.
At the same time, Neighbor said, "Neighbor."
I looked at Neighbor. "Seriously?"
She shrugged. "We're one day apart. We're really not that different. It's not so shocking we decided on the same name for each other."
"I guess not."
Neighbor looked at the Dame. "What do *you* call *me*...?"
"Headache," the Dame grunted.
Neighbor actually looked a little proud of that.

***

After the Dame went back to her own time, Neighbor cooked dinner for us. We watched it in front of the TV, staring at an episode of a British panel show we'd both seen multiple times. She had her feet up on the coffee table, and I stared at her shoes wondering why I was annoyed by that. I did it myself plenty of times. And I did get annoyed if other people did it. But she was me, it was her coffee table, too, and it shouldn't have been any different.

She suddenly uncrossed her ankles and put her feet on the floor.

"Did you do that because~"

"I realized it might be weird," she said. "This is your version of the apartment. I know I would be annoyed if I was watching you do it in my apartment."

I nodded. "Yeah..."

We watched five comedians competing to draw the best circle for a while as we considered the feet-on-table situation.

"It's because we're so close to each other," I said.

Neighbor looked down at the strip of couch cushion between us.

"You know that's not what I meant. We never jump back one day. It's weeks, months, years. The fact that we're only a few hours apart means we're more alike than any other versions of us we've ever met. It's strange. We've had too many of the same experiences and we're more alike than we are different. We're not used to that."

"Makes sense. Is that why we find each other so irritating?"

I looked at her. "I don't find you irritating."

"Really?" She raised her eyebrows, skeptical. "Not even a little bit?"

I sighed and looked at the TV again. "Well, you *are* an unexpected houseguest. That's bound to get on anyone's nerves."

She grunted in agreement. "At least it'll be over soon. You'll rob the bank, we'll split up the cash, and then the Dame will let me go home."

"I look forward to becoming you."

"Technically you already have."

"True." I picked up my drink and offered it to her. "Here's to tomorrow."

She tapped her glass against mine.

Chapter Eight

Still with me? I know all of this is complicated and twisty and confusing. So consider this a second to catch your breath, because in a second it's going to get even worse. Sorry about that. But imagine how I feel! This is my life! I'm constantly driving down a highway at a hundred miles an hour in a car with no windows. At least this time there's someone in the passenger seat telling me when to slow down or change lanes, but I can't even be sure I trust that person.

I can't promise you everything is going to make sense as it happens. I can't say you'll understand what happened because I'm not sure *I* understand it. But I will tell you that it comes together in the end. Hopefully. *I'm* satisfied with how everything shakes out.

But then again, I also try not to think very hard about this stretch of my life. So who knows.

Once more into the breach, as they say. Where were we? I was about to go back to the nineties for the second time to confirm everything I saw on the first visit. The last recon mission before I legitimately became a bank robber.

Let's get back to it.

First National Bank once again stood on Michigan Avenue facing the river on a bright July day in 1990. I retraced my steps across the eventual DuSable Bridge and stopped next to the bridgehouse. This time I was on the other side of the street. I figured getting a slightly different angle on things couldn't hurt. The street was just as busy as it had been the last time I was there. No reason why it wouldn't be. It was the exact same day. Everything was the same, except the day-old version of me wasn't lurking across the street. Sometimes I wondered where those other versions of me went. Those trips still happened. I still remembered them. But suddenly I just wasn't there anymore. It was enough to give someone a crisis if she stopped and thought about it too much.

Luckily I had other things keeping my mind occupied.

I crossed the street and went into the bank. I saw the same tellers behind the same plastic barriers. The same plastic bullets whooshed and swooped through pneumatic tubes set into the walls. My pants were slightly too big and I hitched them up as I walked toward the check-writing station just as I'd done the last time I was here.

"Can I help you, ma'am?"

I turned around. Flirty security guard's voice was sharper now, no hint of the friendliness he'd had before. I'm sure he thought I was a vagrant seeking to get out of the heat for a little while. In anticipation of his attentions, I had center-parted my hair and tied it into uneven pigtails. I wasn't wearing any makeup, and I had dug out an old pair of eyeglasses instead of wearing my contacts. It had taken a little searching to find a sweatshirt in my closet that looked like it could be from the nineties, but I eventually found a vintage Nike shirt that would do the trick.

"Oh I'm waiting for a friend."

He narrowed his eyes. "A friend...?"

I took out two folded hundred dollar bills. "I'm loaning her some cash, and she said she'd meet me here so she could put it into her account right away."

He looked at the money, then back at me. I smiled big, squinting my eyes, and tucked the cash back into my pocket.

"She's probably just running a little late. I'll just wait over there for her, if it's okay."

He looked like he wanted to sweep me back out the door, but the fact I had money meant that I was a potential customer. That was the exact reason I'd switched the alibi. If I had shown up looking like this and claimed I was waiting for someone to bring *me* money, there's no way he would've let me hang around. It was shameful, and I wish there was some way I could rub his face in his prejudices, but alas, I had no proof. The encounter I had yesterday no longer existed, at least not in this timeline. I'd just erased it. But I would always know, and that would have to be enough.

"Fifteen minutes," he said finally.

"Mm-hmm. Absolutely, sure, yes. Thank you very much."

He returned to his chair and I went to the waiting area. I took a different seat from the time before, this one with an angle down the hall leading to the vault. It would be good to know if anyone had been lurking down there during this window.

So I sat, I drummed my fingers, I watched people out the window and examined everyone who came through the door. It made sense that I'd be aware if I was waiting for a friend, but I was just refreshing my mental checklist. Nothing had changed, and the number of people stayed the same.

I thought the only difference would be that the guard would keep his distance. But, just like last time, he came strolling over. He stopped in front of me, thumbs hooked in his belt loops.

"It looks like you've been stood up," he said, his voice flat.

I smiled bashfully up at him. "Guess so. Story of my life." I sighed and shook my head, then stood up. "This is exactly why she's always getting in trouble! So unreliable." Standing had put us uncomfortably close to each other. "Whoopsie, 'scuse me." I shuffled to one side.

He gestured impatiently toward the door.

"Mm-hmm, I'll go." I touched my glasses, then tilted my head. "You know, you're kind of good-looking. When is your break? Maybe I could use some of this money to buy you lunch?"

I could have done without the flicker of disgust that passed over his features. I had dressed to depress, but still. Rude.

"I have a girlfriend."

I blinked at him. Could he be lying? "You what? What's her name?"

He frowned. "What?"

"Your girlfriend. Unless... oh wait, are you lying because you're not interested?"

"Her name is Carolyn," he said, "not that it's any of your business."

I was stunned. He hadn't hesitated at all, which meant... "You're telling the truth. And you were *flirting* with- you asked me out when you had a girlfriend?"

"You asked *me* out!" His confusion was battling with his anger.

"Yeah, *this time*," I snapped, then turned away and stormed toward the exit. "Unbelievable! What a piece of complete trash..."

Outside, I was trying to figure out ways I could find Carolyn and warn her before I went back to the present. I rounded the corner, still so angry that I barely noticed the woman who stepped out of my way so I wouldn't collide with her. She noticed me, however, and grabbed my bicep. I tried to pull away from her, twisting back to see who would have the nerve to-

I was looking into my own face.

"Oh, you've got to be shitting me," I muttered.

She smiled without humor. She didn't look much older than me, but she was basically skin and bones. She undid the top button of her blouse and pulled it down just enough to reveal what could only be a healed bullet wound just below her collar bone.

"Oh, what the fuck?" I whispered.
She pulled her collar back up. "We've got a lot to talk about."

***

We went to a coffeeshop near the bank. She got us two coffees and a croissant to share, while I took a table by the window and covered my face with both hands. Another timeline. Another version of my life. Time traveling was one thing. I had spent my entire life going back and forth and dealing with older and younger selves. That was fine. But now I had to think about duplicates? Completely different versions of myself running around? Including one who had been *shot*?

She sat down across from me. She took a sip of her coffee and relaxed into her seat. "Go ahead and take your time. I know this is a pretty big deal for you."

I dropped my hands and stared at her. "How far ahead of me are you?"

"About a year." She tapped her chest. "This took a while to get over. Lots of hospital time."

"I'm sure," I said. "How did it happen?"

She glared at me. "Remind me what you're planning again...?"

I frowned. "Wait. The others implied this~"

She held up a hand to stop me. "They said they were trying to prevent this idea from sparking other timelines, right? That's why you had to go through with it, even though they pointed out how ludicrous the whole thing was?"

I stared at her.

"They've done this before. I don't know if I was their most recent attempt or if they tried other timelines before getting to you. But when I tried it, I got shot by the guard."

"The asshole who asked me out even though he has a girlfriend?"

"No, I didn't choose this bank," she said. "They think of you - of every version of us they rope into this stupid idea - as the Pawn. They put you in danger and then wait to see if it pays off."

I shook my head. "This is insane. My whole life, every version of myself that I've met has been me. Someone I know and recognize. And now suddenly there are *three* of me?"

"Oh, there are a lot more than three," she said. "And you'd never created a timeline before. You caused a big ol' tear in all our worlds when you created a version of us who knew our mother. The walls are thin and a lot more fragile than we want to believe. Once you break through one, the hole goes both ways. These two, they can sense it. Like bloodhounds. They're determined to make their stupid plan work, and they don't care how many of us they have to go through to get it. And why should they? The universe has an infinite supply of us."

"Is there a way to... uh, unbreak the wall? I just want my life to go back to normal."

"Not that I know of," she said. "I barely know anything about the process. Queen and Clone never exp~"

"That's what you call them?"

She nodded. "What do you call them?"

"Dame and Neighbor."

She shrugged dismissively. "The terrible twosome never explained it to me. They were very cagey about the whole process. Should've been my first red flag."

"Mine too."

She leaned forward with her elbows on the table. "The only option we have is to get them their fucking money. Is this your first or second trip to scout the location?"

"Second. So the next time I'm here, it's on."

"The moment of truth. Feeling confident?"

I looked at her chest. "Well, I *was*. The security guard flirted with me the first time, so I tried to dress as unappealing as possible this time."

"Oh-h, okay. I didn't want to be rude, but I was

wondering."

I narrowed my eyes at her. "Yeah. Well. You look like you could stand to put a little meat on your bones."

"Yeah, I've really been focusing on healing from the gunshot wound the past few months."

Shit. I cringed and leaned back. "Sorry."

She waved it off and looked around the coffeeshop. "So the next time you're here. Any idea when that is going to happen?"

"No clue. I would have assumed tomorrow, just to get it over with. But now that I know the whole story..." I held out my hands. "Why can't I just back out? They've been lying about everything. Why don't I just tell them to hit the highway and find the next chump in line?"

"The next chump will still be you. This version of you has already done two-thirds of the work. It makes sense to go through with it and maybe spare another Chloe Cross from suffering."

"Why should I believe my attempt will go any better than yours?"

She considered that. "Who chose the bank? You or them?"

"Neighbor did. I mean, the younger–"

"Right. So I assume they have a list they're going down." She hooked a thumb over her shoulder at the bank I'd been scouting. "That's not the same one I hit. So when I got shot, I assume that means they crossed that bank off the list for being too risky. Depending on how many times they've done this, you might have a higher chance of success based on process of elimination."

I took a deep breath and blew it out slowly. "I guess no matter what I decide, I'm destined to become a bank robber."

"Seems that way."

"Well, you know what they say." I sighed. "I only have myself to blame."

She laughed and raised her coffee in a toast. "Ain't that always the truth..."

***

I made a pitstop before going home. I had never given a name to the wounded version of me, since her injury was the most defining difference between us and it felt awkward to use that as an identifier. She wished me luck and left me at the coffeeshop to go back to her timeline, where I assumed she was free from the Dame and Neighbor's scheming. I didn't envy her, though. I couldn't imagine how being shot in the chest would've shattered my entire life. Not just being in the hospital and losing work, but it would be devastating mentally and emotionally. I'd never given it much thought before... why would I? Who wants to shoot a chef?

But now that it was in my head, and I'd seen that healed wound on "my" chest, I couldn't stop thinking about it. I didn't want to face any other versions of myself in this headspace so I jumped to a random night in January. I landed in downtown, sometime around ten o'clock at night. It was perfect; I was surrounded by people who weren't me.

I should spend more time with people who weren't me.

By the time I got to Millennium Park, my head was empty enough that I could at least begin to focus my thoughts. The Dame and Neighbor were fucking liars. They were basically going through the neighborhood, knocking on everyone's door, tricking them into trying to rob a bank, and then moving on. Who knew how many of me had died trying to make those two rich? And was Neighbor *really* being held against her will in my timeline? Or was she just there to babysit me? To make sure I played along with their scheme and no one tried to warn me. Maybe that's why the other me waited until I was in the past to spill the beans. I was lucky she'd found me.

Unless *she* was the liar.

But she *did* have a gunshot wound. Someone really had shot her in the chest.

I sighed and walked under the Bean. I tilted my head back and looked at my reflection. The way the glass sculpture was designed, I was reflected multiple times from different angles. I searched for and found every distorted version of myself looking back at me in the curved skin. I took my hands out of my pockets and slowly brought them up, raising my middle finger at each individual Chloe Cross warping in the stainless steel.

I dropped my hands and glared up at my other faces.

"You want to rob a bank?" I muttered. "All right, bitches. Let's rob a fucking bank."

I realize I say that a lot. But if I have to have a catchphrase...

Chapter Nine

"You can't go back four times." The Dame glared at me, arms crossed over her chest. "We went over this and you agreed."

"Well, I'm changing my mind." I also crossed my arms. "I need one more scouting trip before I'm comfortable going in with a weapon."

Neighbor was at the table between us, watching the confrontation with detached interest. She had one elbow on the table, propping up her chin.

"Yesterday you said the bank was quiet. Not too busy. Now you need extra time? Why?"

"Just to be sure. I'm iffy on the security guard. He reacted so differently based on my appearance that I can't be sure how he'll react if I walk in dressed like a robber." We'd decided that I would be wearing a hoodie, oversized jeans held up by a belt, a knit cap, and sunglasses. I figured the Unabomber had gotten away with a similar costume for so many years, it would work for me for a single day. "It's just one more trip. I'm sure you want me to be confident about pulling this off."

The Dame exchanged a look with Neighbor. Before, I would've written it off as just a casual glance. But now that I knew they were conspiring together, I knew they were having some kind of mental conversation. You have no idea how irritating it is to be a third wheel with *yourself*.

"How about this?" Neighbor said. "We agree to a fourth trip if one is necessary. But you go back the third time prepared to go through with the plan if you see an opening."

I considered the compromise. I still had the chance to delay if I didn't get the information I wanted. Once I was in 1990, every call was mine to make. I could back out at any time. And obviously if I came back from the third trip having not robbed the bank, the Dame would have to agree on a fourth trip if she wanted to get her money. I had all the power. I just didn't want to go too rogue without having them on board unless I absolutely had to. These versions of me could jump between timelines whenever they wanted. I didn't want to find out what else that ability entailed.

I was still pretty damn worried about guns, though.

"Okay," I said. "I can work with that."

Neighbor looked at the Dame. "Well?"

She didn't look happy with either of us. Finally she uncrossed her arms and flipped her hands up in surrender.

"Fine. One extra trip, but *only* if it's necessary. The next time you go back, you'll be fully prepared to go through with the robbery."

I nodded. "I can live with that." Hopefully.

Neighbor said, "See? I knew we could all be reasonable. So when do you want to go?"

I had considered that during my pitstop. "Tomorrow morning. I'll get a good night's sleep so I'm completely rested."

"Makes sense," the Dame said.

The plan involved me coming back to the present within five minutes of leaving, so they wouldn't have to wait very long to know if it worked. They wouldn't know how long I spent in 1990 unless I told them, and I had no intention of spilling those particular beans at this juncture.

"Let's all get a good night's sleep before we meet up again," the Dame said. "Look lively, ladies. Tomorrow this whole mess will be over, and all three of us will be a lot richer."

When she put it like that, it was so easy to believe.

***

I didn't particularly want to share the bed with Neighbor that night, but I also didn't want to tip her off that anything had changed. When she tried to initiate sex, I had the excuse that I wanted to preserve my energy for the robbery in the morning. "Like a boxer before a fight, you know?"

She settled back on her side of the bed. "I know that's an urban legend, so I know *you* know it. But all right. You don't have to have an excuse."

"How noble of you," I said, putting my hands under the pillow and staring up at the ceiling.

"You're up to something."

I didn't look at her. I could tell she was laying on her side, facing me, and I didn't want to make eye contact. "Of course I am. I'm planning a bank robbery."

"There's something you aren't telling us about the day."

"There's nothing you need to know that I haven't already told you. I'm the one who needs all the information. And I've got it. I'll be ready."

"After one extra trip."

"One potential extra trip," I said. "Yeah."

She stared at me for a while without saying anything. Then she finally rolled onto her back and put her hands under her pillow as well.

"It'll all be over tomorrow," she said, echoing the Dame's words.

"Yep," I said.

To them, anyway. To me, tomorrow was at least two days' worth of living, and I had to be vigilant to make sure I survived them.

***

First National Bank still stood on Michigan Avenue facing the river in the summer of 1990. The major difference to this trip from my other two visits was that I crossed the bridge just after four-thirty in the morning. The sun still hadn't come up, but I could see it starting to color the eastern sky. As I had promised the Dame, I was dressed to rob the place. I had a gun in my the pocket of my hoodie but it was unloaded. I didn't think that would matter if the case was ever somehow brought to court, but it definitely made me feel more confident about everything I had to do.

The bank opened at five-thirty, but I figured the employees would show up before that to get ready for the day. That was the reason I needed a buffer trip. If I was wrong about when they got to work, or in what order, I would need a do-over. So far things looked good. The bank was still dark and apparently empty. There was a lighted vestibule near the main entrance for a 24-hour ATM, but the main lobby looked abandoned save for security lights along the baseboards.

So I crouched down by the bridgehouse and waited. Another reason I might need another go: if a cop showed up and asked what I was doing, it would be very hard to explain my presence and the gun in my pocket. I was down on one knee, my hands near my foot so if someone did approach, I could lie and say I was just tying my shoes. That might work to get me enough time to make a run for it. I kept my eyes peeled for anyone in a uniform and also watched the bank for any movement.

The first person in a suit arrived at fifteen minutes after five. He wasn't the security guard, and I bit back an annoyed grunt. He unlocked the door, let himself in, and locked the door again behind him. Then he crossed the lobby and disappeared into one of the offices. I only had to wait a few minutes before someone else appeared. She must have entered through a back entrance, because she was already inside when I saw her.

"Shit," I muttered. If the security guard used the same entrance...

No. I spotted him coming down the street with a white paper bag in his left hand, digging through it with his right. He pulled out a doughnut and took a bite, chewing with his mouth open as he strolled toward work. I slipped the gun from my pocket and stood up, stretching my legs to work out any kinks that might've set in while I was waiting. I put on a pair of sunglasses that made it very hard to see, though the sun was higher in the sky by now. The less descriptors people had to work with, the better.

I started walking toward the bank on an intercept course. I matched his speed and gait so we would cross paths before he reached the front entrance of the bank. He was so focused on his breakfast, or maybe distracted by thoughts of cheating, that he didn't notice my approach until I was immediately in front of him. Lousy guard, lousy boyfriend... this guy was a real catch. He blinked in surprise and took a step back, still chewing on his doughnut so he couldn't ask who I was.

I pressed the gun into his stomach and pushed, turning him until his back was against the wall. His eyes went wide and he swallowed hard.

"What the hell, lady?"

"You know, the times we talked, I never got your name." I looked at his tag. "Curtis. First name or last?"

"Wh..."

"It doesn't matter. There's something I need to do, Curtis, and you're going to help me."

He looked toward the bank, then back at me. "You can't be serious. Why would I~"

"Because you don't want Carolyn to find out what you've been up to." He had the audacity to look confused, but I cut off any attempted denials. "How many women did you hit on during your last shift, Curtis? Hm? I assume Carolyn doesn't know about the speed dating games you're playing on the customers who go through here."

He swallowed hard again. "I-I can't... I can't... d-d-do anything. I can't~"

"Can you lock me in the vault?"

He frowned. "What?"

"I want you to walk me in there, take me to the vault, and close the door on me."

"Are you crazy?"

I sighed. "You know, I've considered that. So much of the past few days, I've basically just been talking to myself. But that's been my whole life, really. So maybe I just didn't notice when it really ramped up. Maybe this whole thing is really a brain tumor. Maybe it really is 1990, and I'm just imagining that I'm from thirty years in the future. That would kind of be a relief in a lot of ways." I leaned in and lowered my voice. "Shit's going to start getting *real* crazy, *real* soon. Enjoy the nineties, pal, that's all I'm gonna say about that."

"You *are* crazy."

I shrugged. "Sure, buddy. Maybe I am. I can't confidently deny it, so why not. Which means there's a crazy woman with a gun who is asking you to lock her in the vault. Can you think of a place you would rather have me?"

He looked confused. "You make a pretty good point."

"One more thing. I need you to wait thirty minutes before you call the police."

"What? Why?"

"Thirty minutes. With the vault door shut. There's no other way out of there, so it shouldn't matter. Right?" I pushed the gun harder against his stomach. "It's nice and easy for everyone involved."

"Fine. Yeah. I'll take you."

"Great!" I looked around to make sure we were still alone on the street, then nodded for him to start walking. "Let's go, Curtis."

He cautiously moved away from the wall and started walking. I kept the gun in the small of his back, just reminding him it was there.

"Why- h-how do you know Carolyn?"

"That doesn't really matter."

He said, "I'm not a cheater."

I rolled my eyes. "Spare me. I don't care about your

excuses or what loopholes you jump through to sleep at night. All I care about is getting in that vault."

"I love Carolyn."

"That's great, buddy."

He stopped by the door. "It's not loaded."

My heart jumped into my throat. "What?"

"My gun," he said. "It's not loaded. I didn't want you to think I was... um... I h-have to get my keys out. I'm not going for a gun."

I looked down. There was a holstered gun on his hip.

He'd never had a gun before. That was one of the first things I noticed about him.

"Do you wear that for your entire shift?"

He started to turn around to look at me, then quickly decided to keep facing forward. "Y-yeah? I-it's part of the j-j-job. But it's unloaded, like I said." He was shaking. "C-can I get the keys now?"

"Is there a reason you'd take the gun off during your shift?"

"What does that matter?" He sounded like he was on the verge of panicking. That would be very bad. "I can take it off right now if you want. Leave it outside. But I swear, it's unloaded."

"Unlock the doors," I said.

Curtis got out the keys and, hands trembling, managed to get the door open. My mind was racing. Was it the wrong day? Had I jumped into a different timeline without realizing it? Everything else was right, as far as I knew. I'd never shown up this early before, but I'd gotten enough details right to make Curtis piss his pants.

So why did he have a gun that he'd never had before? Had I just not noticed? Had I somehow cased a bank *twice* and never noticed the guard was armed? How shitty of a bank robber was I?

Curtis looked around the lobby. "J-just straight to the v-v-vault?"

"Yep. Quick as you can. Don't run."

He started walking just as the woman came out of an office behind the teller station. "Hi, Curtis! Did you get my bear claw?" Her smile wavered when she saw me. "Oh! Did you bring a... friend...?"

"Go back in the office, Doreen," Curtis said. "Everything's fine!"

"Oh, lord," Doreen muttered, turning on her heel and scurrying back out of sight.

I grabbed the back of Curtis' collar and used the gun like a yoke. "Go! To the vault! Now!"

He ran. It was hard for me to keep up with him, but I managed. The vault door was standing wide open, the lights on, and I let go of Curtis. He stumbled and fell to one side, and I ran around him. Once I was in the vault, I turned to face him. I waved at the door.

"Close it! Lock me in, and don't let anyone open it for half an hour. You understand?"

He nodded. He looked deathly pale, and I think he might have started crying as he pushed the door shut behind me. I heard someone, probably the suit who was first to arrive, shouting at Curtis to stop. Luckily Curtis didn't pay attention and just kept pushing. A moment later the heavy door closed with what sounded like a *very* decisive click.

I took a second to catch my breath, eyes closed, bending forward with my hands on my knees. My heart was jackhammering in my chest. I'd done it. I was in the vault, locked in, hopefully no cops showing up for a half hour. By that time I hoped I would be long gone and, if that was going to happen, I didn't have time to waste figuring out Curtis' mysterious gun.

I unzipped my hoodie, which I'd been wearing over a backpack. The vault was extremely simple: just bags and boxes of tightly-bound currency sitting on bare shelves. I scanned the corners of the ceiling and saw there was one security camera aimed down at the table in the middle of the space. I scooted a chair over and climbed up, turning the camera until its lens was aimed at the ceiling. I looked for more sophisticated surveillance, but I didn't see anything. 1990 wasn't the dark ages, but I figured anything they had would be noticeable.

Convinced I had blinded them, I jumped down. There was a literal fortune all around me, and I could only take as much as would fit in a JanSport. I put the bag on the counting table in the middle of the room, unzipped it, and got to work filling it up.

Chapter Ten

I was robbing a bank.

I was a bank robber.

After I filled the bag with as much money could comfortably fit, and making sure I could still carry it, I zipped it closed and looked at the vault door. I thought I could hear voices outside but accepted that it might've just been paranoia. It was the same reason that, while I'd been filling the bag, I thought about how I had never time-traveled from inside a room this secure. What if there was something about the thickness of the walls that kept me from jumping?

I was sweating under my layers of clothes when I finally decided it was time to go. I decided I wasn't going to follow the Dame's rules. So what if I ended up in the vault again when I landed? I could just jump to another time until I ended up outside. If she could screw up various timelines for her plan to work, then I could take as many tries as necessary to escape. I wasn't going to risk getting shot by Curtis when I was born with a built-in escape hatch.

I closed my eyes on focused on my exit point. I always

landed near myself, so I figured I just had to choose a time when I wasn't in Chicago. May 3, 2019, I was in Fort Wayne, Indiana, for a friend's wedding. I took a deep breath and...

...opened my eyes in a dark hotel room. For a second I panicked, thinking I was still inside the vault, but I adjusted to the darkness enough to see a window in the corner. I heard something behind me and turned to see a dark shape in the shadows. A bed, and someone sitting up in it.

"Hey, is that you?" another version of me whispered.

"Yeah. Sorry. Just making a little detour."

"Everything okay?"

I said, "Everything's... uh, yeah. Nothing for you to worry about that."

Sleepy knew how to read between those lines, and she also knew not to press too hard. "Okay. Do you need a place to sleep?"

"No, I'm hopping right back out again. But hey... listen. You leave tomorrow, right?"

"Yeah."

"That hot bridesmaid wants you to make a move. She doesn't tell you until an email six months from now, which does *nothing* for *nobody*. Find her in the morning and make the most of the day."

She sat up farther. "Are you trying to change the future? You know that it won't change what happened to you~"

I waved my hands before she could scold me. I'd had enough of this timeline shit to last all my lifetimes. "I know, I know, but all versions of me deserve to get laid."

"Thanks. See you in a few years."

I smiled even though she wouldn't see it. "Sweet dreams."

A second later, I was back in Chicago, back in 2024. My backpack still hung heavy on my shoulders, full with a small fortune. I took a deep breath and looked around to get my bearings, then started walking. I took out my phone to check the time and confirmed that I had, as planned, arrived eight minutes after I left. See, earlier I said it was hard to pin down my age even though I knew the exact minute I was born. Pop back into the past, see a concert, come home in time to get a full night's sleep. Sometimes I had thirty-six hour days. Sometimes I only saw dawn and sunset of a given calendar day. It was very confusing.

I had almost made it to the stairs of the El station when I suddenly became dizzy. Not just dizzy. Like I'd been nailed to the ground but someone picked up the rest of the world and gave it a few hard shakes. I fell sideways and bumped into someone on my way to lean against a wall. I managed a garbled, "Excuse me," and flattened my hand against the wall like I was clinging to driftwood in a whirlpool. The other person didn't seem to feel the same quake, so I accepted it was due to something I'd done.

Memories from the wedding flooded my mind. I remembered waking up and seeing another version of myself in my room. I remembered the advice to go find the bridesmaid. And I'd done it. The next morning I found her at the hotel gym and asked if she wanted to use the shower in my room. "I think we all have the same showers, right?" she'd said with a flirtatious smile. I had just shrugged and said that maybe mine had some interesting features that she wouldn't find in hers.

And we did go to my hotel room. She showered. I showered. And the two of us might have had the most fun anyone has ever had in Fort Wayne, Indiana.

"I shouldn't remember that," I whispered.

I had changed what happened that day, which meant showering with the bridesmaid should have happened to another version of me. I shouldn't know her name was Bobbi, short for Roberta, and she had flown in from New Hampshire for the wedding. I shouldn't remember just over a year of trying to make a long-distance relationship work before she dumped me for someone local.

My heart pounded. The only explanation was that I'd jumped into the wrong timeline again. But the new memories forming in my mind... that hadn't happened last time. This felt more organic. Like the world around me was literally changing because of what I'd done.

I swallowed the lump in my throat and pushed away from the wall. My dizziness had faded but it took a few more seconds before I trusted my legs to support me.

"Are you okay?"

I smiled toward the voice and smiled in what I hoped was a reassuring way. "Just a little, um, migraine. They spike me hard sometimes. I'm fine now."

"If you're sure..."

I hurried past the good Samaritan before he insisted on helping further. I got up the stairs in time to catch the train. Fortunately it was the right train to get me back to my apartment. I took off the backpack and set it in my lap, wrapped my arms around it. I had no idea how much money I'd gotten away with. I had just grabbed the bundles off the shelf and threw it into the bag until I ran out of room. I didn't even know if I had grabbed hundreds or twenties. Or, God forbid, singles. There would be enough time to count it later.

The thought of 'enough time' tripped my over-tired, exhausted, confused brain, and I started laughing. The adrenaline of the bank robbery was also burning off, and the residue was making me feel hysterical. I knew I was 'that person' on the train... the one dressed weird, the one hunched over her bag, the one laughing like a psychopath at a joke only I could hear, but I didn't care. Let them be scared of me. At least the thieves would steer clear along with everyone else.

That just made me laugh harder. Me! The bank robber worried about getting mugged!

I didn't stop laughing until I got to my stop. I was out of breath but I managed to find the strength to get home. I unlocked the door and stepped inside like I had just run the entire way from the bank with the cops hot on my tail. The Dame was at the dinner table, where I'd left her, and she got to her feet as I came in.

She followed the bag with her eyes until I dropped it on the table. She stared for a second, then looked at me with her eyebrows raised.

"I assume this means everything went to plan?"

"More or less," I said, dropping heavily into a chair.

She unzipped the bag and started taking out stacks of cash. I watched for a few seconds, then scanned the rest of the apartment. It wasn't a very big place, so it didn't take long.

"Where's Neighbor?"

"Who?"

"The other me. The younger--" I waved my hand generally next to me. "The one you're conspiring with. The one who came up with this whole idea."

The Dame stopped pulling bundles and looked at me. "This was *your* idea."

"No," I said. "Another version of me, a version one day older than me, showed up and tried to talk me into it. But then *you* showed up and said we had to go through with it so other timelines wouldn't get the same idea and ruin..." I narrowed my eyes at her. She looked completely confused. "There have been three of us planning this from the beginning."

"It's only been you and me," she said. "There's no 'Neighbor' version."

"What do you call me?"

"Headache."

My heart leapt into my throat. "No... that's what you called *her*."

"There is no *her*," my older version said.

I stood up. "I'm in the wrong timeline."

"That isn't possible."

"To get out of the vault, I went to 2019 when I was at a wedding in Indiana. I changed what happened by telling her to hook up with a hot bridesmaid. As soon as I got back, I remembered that happening. I remembered fucking the bridesmaid, and the relationship we had afterward."

The Dame looked tense. "Was that the first odd thing you noticed?"

I had to think for a second, but then I remembered. "The security guard at the bank had a gun. He'd never had a gun before, on the other trips."

"You're sure?"

"Number of weapons in the room tends to be one of the first things you check when you're robbing a place."

"And you're positive it was the same day as before?"

I started to answer affirmatively, but I stopped myself. Sometimes I'd been off by a few hours. Arriving so early in the morning might have affected my landing. But no. I also had a pretty solid sixth sense about knowing when I was, and there hadn't been any alarm bells ringing when I arrived. I'd landed on the right day, just a few hours earlier than my first two trips.

"It was the right day," I insisted.

The Dame thought for a second, then looked around. "Where's your computer?"

I went to the desk and turned on my laptop. She sat down and opened a browser, typing in the bank's name, 1990, and robbery. I loomed over her and watched as the results popped up.

"Oh, shit," we said together.

MYSTERIOUS BANK ROBBERY STILL MYSTIFIES 30 YEARS LATER

BANK-ROBBING GHOST VANISHES INTO THIN AIR

WHERE DID SHE GO? AND THEN WHERE DID SHE GO??

"This shouldn't be here," the Dame said, her voice rough.

"I thought you said it would make a new branch. A new timeline~"

"It was supposed to!" she snapped, pushing away from the desk so fast that the chair hit me in the gut. She stood and turned to face me. "You must have done something wrong."

"I went exactly according to the plan."

"And you're certain there was a third version of us here when you left?"

I rolled my eyes. "Yeah, she was here. We slept together, we fucked, it's not exactly something I would hallucinate. You insisted she stay here instead of jumping back and forth to her own timeline while we were planning."

She started pacing. "That's not good. That means you *did* create new branches. The bank robbery, the bridesmaid, the guard having a gun. But if you actually remember them, if there's evidence that they happened to this version of you, then it means the timelines are collapsing into each other."

That made me feel very cold, very quickly. "Okay. What does *that* mean?"

"It's not the end of the world," she said. "Not... literally."

"Not comforting. How can we stop it?"

She crossed her arms over her chest. "We can't."

There was a knock on the apartment door. I turned to look, then looked at the Dame.

"Don't look at me," she said. "You're the one insisting we're a trio."

I went to the door and rested my hand on the knob. I didn't want to look through the peephole and confirm my fear that I'd see a whole SWAT team of people ready to arrest me for a crime that had happened when I was two years old. I took a deep breath. I let it out slowly. And praying my voice would sound normal, said, "Who is it?"

"It's your mother. Open the door. I'm here to fix what you fucked up."

Chapter Eleven

My mother stormed into the apartment, ignoring my shocked look. She was around my age, which made it weird to see her. It was even weird to see her fixing a Mom Glare at a version of me that was so much older than her. The Dame actually seemed to shrink under my - her - mother's gaze. I guess that sort of thing never really goes away. I had gotten it from my foster parents, sure, but there was something different about judgement from the person who gave you life. That's blood judgement, and there's no growing out of anxiety from that.

I swallowed hard and looked at my older self. She had walked past the Dame and was leaning down to look at the laptop. She typed for a second, shaking her head.

"These things are unbelievable," she said under her breath. "Where I'm from, you'd have to be rich to have a computer in your house. You've got this one, plus another one in your damn pocket, and you're poor as hell."

"Hey! I'm not doing that bad, thank you." I pointed at the table. "Not to mention--"

Mom snorted. "Yeah. About that... have fun trying to spend it." She straightened up and pointed at the screen. "So. You're infamous."

The Dame and I moved closer to the laptop. She'd opened a YouTube video and clicked PLAY.

I recognized the voice of the journalist who started talking, but I couldn't think of her name. "On an otherwise ordinary July morning in 1990, Curtis Reed arrived to work at the First National Bank of Chicago the same as any other day. But this morning... *someone* was *waiting* for him."

On screen I watched grainy security footage of myself as I hurried across the street from the bridge and intercepted Curtis and pushed him up against the wall. It was too dark to see many details. He stopped and turned to face me. Anyone watching would've thought we were friends who happened to run into each other right before dawn. After what felt like ages, we moved away from the wall and started walking together toward the bank.

"Reed described the woman as dark-haired, middle-aged–"

I blinked but managed to resist offense at that.

"–and quote, 'normal-looking'."

A voiceover I recognized as Curtis said, "She was just like a normal mom, you know?"

"What the hell, I'm thirty-three," I muttered. "Ish."

Curtis continued. "She pulls out this gun and at first I thought it was a joke, you know? Who pulls out a gun and, like, literally says 'I'm gonna rob your bank'? I didn't think she was actually gonna shoot me. But, you know, they tell you to... go along with it, right? Your life is worth more than the money. So I just went along with it."

The journalist picked up again. "But it wasn't a joke. The woman led Curtis Reed into the bank, where she proceeded to give him a very unusual set of instructions."

"She didn't say 'don't call the cops'," Curtis said. "She told me lock her in the vault and wait thirty minutes to send up the alarm. And I'm like, there's no back door in there, honey. You know? But hey, if she wants to be locked in a room by herself, that's keeping everyone safe, so I did what she said."

The bank's security footage continued, showing me lead Curtis across the lobby.

"Curtis did as instructed," the journalist said. "He locked the robber in the vault. Once inside—" The image switched to the vault camera. "—the robber changed the angle of the only security camera so it was aimed at the wall. And that..." Dramatic pause. "...was the last anyone has ever seen of her."

"My manager said it was probably smart to follow her instructions and do what she said, you know?" Curtis said. "So we waited half an hour and called the cops. They show up, and it's crazy. Just, like, insanity. They have a whole army there and they surround the vault door. They open the vault door and it's just... it's, like, it's just *empty*." He laughed. "Poof! Gone. Like she was never there."

"Except she *was* there," the journalist said. "The robber wasn't the *only* thing to vanish during that half hour. An inventory of the vault revealed that two hundred and ninety thousand dollars had also disappeared without a trace."

The Dame, my mother, and I all looked at the backpack. I guess the documentary had just saved us some counting. When we looked back at the screen, the security camera footage had given way to a shot of the journalist walking on the DuSable Bridge.

"Suspicion immediately fell upon Curtis Reed. Police had only his word that the woman was armed. No fingerprints were found in the vault, and only one other employee at the bank reported seeing the woman when Curtis came into the bank."

"I'm so lucky Doreen was there, you know?" Curtis laughed nervously. Now, instead of a voiceover, there was footage of him sitting awkwardly on a couch. He was wearing a dress shirt with a collar so stiff it had to be brand-new. He had aged since the robbery, and I wondered how many years later the interview had been filmed. "If it wasn't for her and the security cameras, it would've been an easy mystery to solve.

Just blame the security guard, right? Luckily I had the proof."

"No evidence was ever found connecting Reed to the crime," the journalist said. "But if he wasn't involved, then who was the woman? Police reviewed security footage from buildings in a one-mile radius surrounding the bank and, in addition to disappearing into thin air, investigators were also never able to find her approaching on that fatal morning."

Curtis said, "It's creepy, you know? Like... she just appeared on the bridge? And then disappeared into thin air? I talked to her, I was standing, like, right next to her, I know she was real. But at the same time, like... I don't know, I kind of believe in ghosts now."

"Many in Chicago feel the same." The journalist stopped and folded her hands in front of her. "In the three decades since the robbery, no sign of the mystery thief has ever been found. The money itself has never been flagged, which implies not a single bill has ever been spent. It would be easy to say it was just an accounting error. It would be easy to claim that the bank manager stole the money in the dead of night and this story was concocted to cover his tracks."

The scene changed to the journalist standing in the bank vault.

"But the woman on the security cameras exists. The money has never turned up in any transactions for the past thirty years. The money was there one minute, and gone the next. Unlike the infamous DB Cooper case, there aren't vast stretches of wilderness to search. Investigators don't have to ask questions about velocity, air speed, flight plans, timing. Everything happened right here, in a vault in the middle of the third-largest city in America.

"The FBI may have stopped actively searching for her, the case may be unofficially closed, but one thing is for certain: Chicago will never stop asking 'What happened to the FN Phantom?'"

I blinked and looked at Mom. "Did she just call me the F'ing Phantom?"

"The F-N Phantom," she said, closing the laptop. As in

First National. But... yeah, a lot of people have used your version, too."

The Dame said, "This was planned for. We always planned to take the money to other timelines where the robbery didn't happen to spend it."

"The fact is that you shouldn't *have* to do that," Mom said. "The robbery should never have happened in Chloe's reality. It should have created a new branch while hers remained untouched." She poked a finger into the laptop. "The fact that the robbery happened in the same timeline where she did it is a big, big problem. Have either of you noticed inconsistencies in the world since you started planning this thing?"

I said, "Curtis had a gun this morning. On the robbery day, I mean. He never had a gun before. I was positive about that. But this time, he did."

Since I'd already spilled the beans, the Dame admitted, "Headache here claims there was a third version of us involved in the planning. She was one day older and from a different timeline."

Mom looked angry but not surprised. "Like I said, the timelines are collapsing into each other. I'm not surprised that one with a twenty-four hour difference would get blended first." She looked at me. "Your third version didn't disappear. You *are* her. If you sit down and think about it, you'll remember the past few days from both point of views."

"I don't think I'm going to think too hard about it right now."

"Smart," Mom said. "Chloe went back to the same day too many times, too close together, and they started to tie together. The reality where Curtis was armed wrapped around one where he wasn't. And they're all still twisting, twisting, tighter and tighter."

"Well, what exactly does that mean?" I was trying not to panic. "It sounds bad."

She started to speak, then sighed and shrugged. "It's not great. But honestly, to you? Other than a few strange memory issues, you'll be fine. You'll remember things that didn't actually happen, you'll forget things that did. Because in this new reality, you won't have done them."

The Dame was back at the table, looking down at the bag of money. "The video said the FBI had closed the case. They're not investigating it anymore, right?"

"You can bet the case will get red hot the second any of those bills shows up in circulation," Mom said. "Especially these days, with computers and digital whatevers. There might be feds outside before you even leave the store. If they get a hint the FN Phantom has finally resurfaced, they'll jump on it like mice on cheese."

"So we'll take it to another timeline," the Dame said.

"Haven't you fucked over enough timelines for one day?" Mom snapped.

The Dame flinched and looked away.

"If you'd been listening, that won't matter. Take it wherever you want, eventually that timeline will fold up into this one and Chloe will end up with the same problem. It's only a matter of time before that bank robbery always occurs in a timeline where she has the money."

A horrible thought was starting to dawn on me. "We have to get rid of it, don't we."

"Unless you want to make headlines as the most infamous bank robber in history," Mom said. "Even if you go with your story about finding it buried in a wall, there will be far too many questions. Where was the wall, who owned the building, who lived there in 1990? Nothing you come up with would hold water. The only option would be to tell the truth."

I laughed. "Time travel."

"And after that, it's hello scientists and testing facilities."

"Or a mental institution," I said.

Mom shrugged and nodded.

"So what do we do?"

Mom went to the bag and zipped it up. "We burn it."

"You know a place where we can burn this amount of money without drawing a whole lot of attention?"

She said, "I do, actually. It's not far from here. I'll give you directions."

I was skeptical, but I nodded.

"After all this, we're just going to *burn* it all?" The Dame closed her eyes. "God, that can't be our only option."

"Oh, you have other options," Mom said. "The other options are going to jail, or becoming a lab rat. Which one of those are you leaning toward, Grandma?" She picked the bag up by the strap and held it out to me. "I trust you to do the right thing with this, Chloe."

I took the bag and let it hang down next to my leg. "And then life can go back to normal?"

"Relatively, anyway," Mom said. "Timelines will keep crashing into each other for a while longer, so I would avoid any traveling for a week or two. But then it will settle down. *If* you are very careful and smarter about your jumping."

"I'm sorry."

She shook her head. "Don't be. I'm as much to blame as you are. It was my responsibility to teach you how to do this shit. I'll do better."

"You did fine," I said quietly.

She smiled. "Thanks, sweetie."

I looked at the Dame. "Before we finish this, there's something I have to know. You and Nei~ well, I guess just you now. This was all a scam, right? You'd done this before. Multiple timelines. Throwing other versions of yourselves to the wolves until you found one that worked."

She looked confused, then surprised. "When did you figure it out?"

"I didn't. One of your pawns tracked me down and let me know the truth."

Mom looked between us, then faced the Dame. "You let my daughter get killed?"

"I *am* your daughter."

Mom reached out and slapped her, hard. Then she looked at her hand, turned to me, and said, "Does that count as child abuse? She's like twice my age."

"I think it's a gray area. Besides, she definitely deserved it."

The Dame sniffed and rubbed her cheek. "It was a means to an end. Plenty of us left."

"A lot less now than there used to be." Mom was still rubbing her hand. "Who knew slapping someone hurt so much? Damn."

I lifted the strap of the bag onto my shoulder. "So should we just get it over with?"

"As soon as she goes home," Mom said. "If she still can. The way branches are collapsing, it might already be gone. Nothing to be done about it."

The Dame legitimately look frightened by that. She looked at me and, with an expression even I couldn't read, said, "See you in a couple of decades, kid."

She was gone in a blink.

I was left alone with Mom and a couple hundred thousand dollars. It was a weird situation. I scratched the back of my neck and motioned at the door.

"Want to come with me? Make sure I actually follow through with it?"

"I trust you."

"It's a lot of money. You're saying you wouldn't be tempted?"

She started to answer, then shrugged. "Okay."

I led the way out of the apartment and we walked downstairs together. I had a thousand things I wanted to ask her, but there didn't seem to be a natural way into the conversation. There was a whole ocean of things I needed to know but without an ice-breaker, I'd never get to them. She was the one who broke the silence as we walked out of the building into the sunlight.

"So I assume something happens to me."

I was startled enough that I flinched away from her. "Why would you say that?"

"Given the way you looked at me when I walked in. Plus, if I'd been around, I would have taught you a few things that would've prevented this from happening."

I nodded. "Yeah. It would be nice to have gotten a rulebook or something. I figured out most of the basics. Wherever I jump, I land within a few miles of wherever I was in that–" I realized something and stepped in front of her. "You're alive."

She tilted her head at me, confused. "What do you mean?"

I gestured at her. "You're here now, in 2024. That means you must be *alive* in 2024. Otherwise you couldn't have landed here."

She blinked. "That's not a rule."

"Of course it's a rule."

"Says who?"

I started to answer, then closed my mouth. Who *had* told me that? It was such a firm rule in my mind that I couldn't remember a time when I hadn't considered it set in stone.

"Time travelers can only travel within their own lifetime. That's fact."

Mom thought for a second, then narrowed her eyes. "That's *Quantum Leap*."

"That's..." I closed my mouth again. I remembered the narration from the show. "Son of a bitch, it's *Quantum Leap*."

She laughed and started walking again. "There are worse shows you could've taken guidelines from. Except he was changing history left and right, and it constantly affected his own timeline. That would've been a mess to sort out."

"So I *can* travel outside my own lifetime."

"It's not advisable," she said. "Best to consider it a very strong suggestion. Going too far either way gets really complicated, really fast."

I sighed. "Complicated enough already."

"Exactly." She glanced at me. "You're beautiful, you know. I'm glad we can travel outside of our lifetime if it means I get to see how you ended up. Lovely young lady with a great job. I'm proud of you, Chloe."

I probably blushed. Pride or self-worth or something

billowed up in my chest.

"Even if you don't have a girlfriend."

I laughed. "And just like that, I see what it's like having a mother."

She bumped my arm with her elbow. "Take your time. And I'm not saying that in an ironic way. She's out there somewhere, and you'll find each other when you're supposed to."

"Thanks, Mom."

"You're welcome, Chloe."

I looked around, wondering where she could be leading me. "I don't know if you're aware of this, but burning anything out in the open is extremely prohibited. There are environmental issues. When I was worried about attention, I was talking about the authorities. The amount of cash we have to burn through, someone will call the cops and the fire department and, I dunno, the EPA before the bag is even half empty."

"We're not going to be setting the fire," Mom said. "We're taking it somewhere we can send it back farther than I've ever gone. Farther than I'd ever care to go."

"We're going to send the money back in time? To..." My eyes widened. "*The* fire...?"

"October 8, 1871. It's kind of poetic, in a way. The FN Phantom is one of Chicago's biggest mysteries, and the solution is buried in the ashes of its history."

I shook my head. "Unbelievable."

She pointed. "We're not far from one of the neighborhoods that burned to the ground. We'll hop back, drop the money, maybe spill some flammable material over it just to be on the safe side, and come home. Problem solved. Your crime is covered up by the literal destruction of a city."

"You never explained where we're going to land. I've always thought I was anchored to wherever I happened to be. But I wasn't around in the eighteen hundreds, so~"

She said, "If you exist in the time you jump to, then you're anchored. But if you go outside your lifetime, you can just kind of... aim yourself. We'll arrive at the same place we left. That's why we're actually walking to a specific spot before we go."

"Makes sense, I guess. And you're not worried about this screwing up the timeline or creating new branches?"

She shook her head. "Far too small an impact. This amount of ash added to an entire mountain of ashes, just one more pile of paper destroyed along with half of Chicago."

"Cash isn't paper."

She looked at me.

"It's, like... I don't know, linen or something. It's not paper."

"Oh," she said. "Okay."

"Sorry. That's pedantic." I looked at the cash. "I still think it's a shame."

"I know, sweetie." She slung an arm across my shoulders. "But trust me, it's for the best."

I put my arm around her waist. I focused on that fact, that I was walking down the street with my mother. Not that long ago, I didn't even know what she looked like. Now I was walking down the street with her after she swooped in to save me from a mess of my own making. What were mothers for, if not that very thing? I smiled and looked at her, memorizing her profile, trying to pick out things I recognized from my own face.

When she felt my eyes on her, she turned and smiled. "What?"

"Nothing," I said, though I was smiling like an idiot. "I was just thinking something really corny."

"Oh! Now you *have* to tell me."

I laughed. "I was just thinking that the past few days have been completely insane. Just one madness after another, after another. But if that was the cost... well, that, and almost three hundred thousand dollars... if that's the price to be here, right now, with you? I'd call that a bargain."

She laughed as well and kissed my hair. "I think that's just below the line for too corny. Thanks, sweetie."

"You're welcome, Mom."

I reveled in how good it felt to say that, smiling as we went to burn the small fortune I'd risked my life to acquire.

I bet you think I forgot about Darwin. I didn't. I'm getting to Darwin and the punch in the face, trust me. I'm just making sure you remember. A lot of stuff has happened since then. But now that we've gotten the bank robbery, the Dame, my Mom's reappearance, and the collapsing timelines out of the way, we can finally get to Darwin. Which is all a long way of saying, as a comedian once said...

I told you that story so I could tell you this story.

PART II
MY LIFE AS A FAILED BANK ROBBER

CHAPTER TWELVE

I quickly realized that while it was *possible* to jump back farther than my lifetime, there were definitely reasons not to.

Most of my jumps happened so quickly and with such little effort that I never really thought of it as being transported. But going back over a hundred years was *definitely* a different experience entirely. My vision blacked out, there was no air, and I had no sense of time in a darkness that felt like hours. It could actually have *been* hours, there's literally no way of knowing for sure. When the world finally came into focus around us again, I immediately fell over like a chopped-down tree. Mom kept me from hitting the ground and patted my back until I could stand on my own.

"I forgot you weren't used to long trips. It's something you just have to get used to."

"I think I'll pass, thanks," I grunted.

The air reeked of smoke. Thick, putrid, an ashy stench that I'll never completely forget. The fire hadn't yet reached the building we were in, but it was clear that this building wouldn't be standing very long. Mom took the bag from me and unzipped it. She turned it upside down and began dumping all that wonderful cash out on the floor. While she did that, I looked around and came back with lighter fluid for a lantern. We splashed it all over the money and stood back. By then, the windows were lighting up with the flickering flames.

"I guess this is probably it," I said.

"Looks like." Mom put her hands on my shoulders and stared hard at me. "I really am proud of you, Chloe. Never doubt that."

I blinked back tears and hugged her. She had abandoned me. She had left me alone, afraid, uncertain, unprepared for a life no one would ever understand. But she was my mother. And she'd come from a place where she actually *did* do the right thing. I'd spent my entire life angry at an abstract version of her. Now, seeing her as a real person, I only felt a swell of love.

"Thanks for saving me, Mom."

"Any time, darling." She stepped back and cupped my face. "Now go back home and just live your life. No more heists or schemes."

I nodded. "No more schemes."

"Good girl." She kissed my forehead and then stepped back. "See you in a few minutes."

I smiled. That sounded so nice, but it also made me realize I'd probably never see her again. I lifted my hand in farewell, and she vanished. I took a deep breath, then coughed violently from all the smoke in the air. My body's instinct was to run, so I turned and took a few stumbling steps before my brain took over and hurtled me back to the right time.

I fell for real this time, tripped over my feet, and landed hard on my stomach. I was so dazed that I was literally seeing stars and little birdies swirling around my head. I coughed hard, a painful sounding retching that should have made anyone in a three-block radius turn and go the other way. Instead, a pair of shoes moved into my line of vision.

The occupant of the shoes crouched down. I looked up

and saw that she was a blurry blob of color, mostly blocked by the sun, but she was holding out a tall reusable water bottle.

"Take it," she said.

I managed to push myself up enough to take her offering. I took a long drink. Water has never tasted so cold, so wonderfully magical. I finished, gasping, and held the bottle out to her.

"Keep it. You need it more than I do." She put her hand on my shoulder. "Come here. There's a little wall you can sit on until you catch your breath."

She guided me over to the low brick wall. I sat down and she sat next to me. I took another sip of her amazing water.

"What is this, filtered or something?"

"Just tap." There was a smile in her voice. "I didn't even see where you came from. It's like you just escaped from a burning building."

I cough-laughed and took another drink. "I kind of did."

I finally looked at her. Her head was tilted back and she was looking at the buildings around us trying to find smoke.

"No, it wasn't here."

"Oh."

"It was 1871."

She stopped looking for smoke. "Pardon?"

"You know, the fire. The big one. Mrs. O'Leary's cow." I took another drink. My throat was starting to feel much better. I gave another cough just to clear the pipes a little. "I was, um. I was back there. With my mother. Who died, or disappeared, I guess, when I was ten. We had to burn a bunch of money I stole."

"Oh," she said again. "So you're... what... a time traveler?"

"Uh-huh," I said.

She was quiet.

I laughed and shook my head. "Fuck. I don't know why I just said that."

"So it's not true."

"No, no, it's definitely true. I'm a time traveler. I just never tell people, because it's a huge can of worms. Scientists and everything." I finished the water in her bottle and held it out to her. "Thank you for that. I really appreciate it."

She took the bottle. "No problem. Are you sure you're okay?"

I nodded. "Mm-hmm. Physically okay and..." I tapped my temple. "No worries. Just forget all that stuff I said. I'm really confused right now."

I stood up and straightened my coat, then started walking away.

"I always thought she got a bad rap."

"What?" I turned around. "Who?"

"Mrs. O'Leary. And her cow." She had crossed one leg over the other, staring at her water bottle like she was reading something off the side. "It's just as likely there were a bunch of drunk guys playing poker in the barn, one of them knocked over the lantern, whole place goes up in flames. But do any of them get the blame for destroying Chicago? Of course not. Mrs. O'Leary goes down in infamy."

I couldn't quite understand what she was getting at. "Uh. The fire was already... I-I didn't see how it started."

"You can't go back and sneak a peek?"

"Probably not the best idea."

She nodded and stood up. She walked up to me and tapped her water bottle against her thigh.

"So, time traveler. Do you have an hour free for dinner with me tonight?"

I frowned at her. "What?"

"Like a date."

"With you?"

"Preferably."

She smiled.

It was a very nice smile.

I shrugged. "I think I can find the time."

"Time travel joke?" she said.

"I've got a million of 'em."

"I bet you do." She put her water bottle into her bag, exchanging it for a phone. "I'll give you my number, we can figure something out."

It sounded like a good plan.

A girl's gotta eat, right?

***

Her name was Stephanie Keith. Once I had a chance to get my head straight - apparently jumping a century can leave you with a hell of a hangover - I realized that she was *very* pretty. A few years older than me, short dark hair, strong jaw. Hazel eyes and a crooked smile. She was really thin and really muscular. Probably either a swimmer or a runner. The kind of woman I would normally admire and walk away from because no way would she have ever been interested in me. And that's on a *good* day, on my *best* day. Why she would ever have asked me out after the day I'd just had, I would never understand.

But the daze had left me defenseless and apparently we had made a date. I kept looking at the text thread we'd created on my phone. She had given me a number to text when I was free, and I had debated for the entire walk home about how to start a conversation. I talked with people almost every day. Conversations were easy to start.

I waited until I was home, showered, and my nerves had settled before I looked at the number and decided to just get it over with. I typed out the text and sent it without giving myself a chance to overthink what I should say or how I should say it.

"Texting you as promised. This is the lady who escaped a fire that you gave water to."

"You'll have to be more specific. I saved like six smoldering women this afternoon alone."

Oh, great, she was an asshole, too. A funny asshole. I was a sucker for funny assholes.

"This is the time traveler."

"Oh right, that does narrow it down. Still smoking?"

"I think it's finally out."

"Well, that's a relief."

I told her about a Thai restaurant within walking distance that I swore by. She hadn't heard of it, but was willing to give it a chance. We figured out a time that worked for both of us and locked it in. I put the phone down and stared at it for a long time. Who was this person? I'd met her one, extremely brief time. I didn't even have a picture to put in my phone for her contact information. And she already knew a secret that I hadn't told *any* of my previous long-term partners. That's like telling someone about your deepest darkest kink on the first date.

But she wasn't running away. And she didn't seem scared off.

I chewed my bottom lip.

Today, I had robbed a bank, discovered I was a legendary mystery figure in Chicago folklore, spent some quality time with my mother, learned a new way to use my time travel powers, actually witnessed the Great Chicago Fire. It was a hell of a day. Might as well end it with a nice meal with an interesting woman.

I forced myself up off the couch and went to take another shower, just to make sure I'd gotten all the smoke smell out of my hair.

***

I got to the restaurant first. I didn't know if the proper etiquette was to be seated, get a drink, and wait. I had been on plenty of dates in the past. Hell, I'd witnessed hundreds of people on dates at Trilogy. You'd think all that research would have led to me being an expert. But I couldn't help thinking that being at the table, drink in hand, would make her feel like she was late. The alternative was to pace around outside looking like a total idiot until she showed up.

Naturally, I chose the latter.

Fortunately I didn't have to wait too long before she came strolling down the sidewalk toward me. She lifted her hand when she spotted me, taking longer strides when she reached the crosswalk. She had changed into a long-sleeved shirt, and I hid my disappointment that I wouldn't get to look at her arms while we ate. She gave me a smile, though, and that almost made up for it.

"Hi! Hope you haven't been waiting long."

"Nope. Just got here myself."

"Good, good."

We were seated at a cramped two-top. When the waiter had departed with our drink orders, she leaned forward with a conspiratorial smile.

"Okay. I think I figured out a way to prove your story."

"Hit me."

She said, "What do you need to know to get to a specific place?"

"Date, time. I can't guarantee location. I usually just end up somewhere around Chicago."

"Perfect." She took out a pen and wrote something on a napkin. She passed it to me.

"November 13, 2002. 3 pm, Our Lady of..." I looked at her. "What's this?"

Her eyes were shining with mischief and excitement. "I want you to go there and tell me what happened."

"Seriously?"

Her smile wavered. "Oh god. Is this insensitive? Or... I'm sorry." She sat up straighter. "I thought it would be fun. But if I crossed a line–"

"No, it's not that." I looked at the note again. "I've just never really talked about what I can do with people. I don't know where the line is, either. If there even *is* a line. But I think this is pretty reasonable. It's a lot to take on faith, and for all you know, I could be a complete psychopath. Going here will prove what I'm saying is true?"

"Well..." She looked suddenly unsure. "Yes. It was never in the newspapers and when I googled, I didn't find anything online about it. So I don't think you could just search on your phone."

I pushed my chair back and stood up. "I'll do it."

Her eyes widened. "Right here?"

"I was going to go in the bathroom."

She looked over her shoulder, then back to me. "You really don't have to."

"No, I want to. I really appreciate you willing to take it on faith and believing me. But I want to reward your trust." I held up the paper. November, Our Lady of Grace. What is this, a girls' school?"

"Yeah..."

"Okay. I'll be right back."

I went to the bathroom. It was a tiny little room, cheaply painted bright red, with a toilet and a sink under a small fogged window. I was hesitant to jump again so soon after traveling with Mom. But it would be a quick trip and I meant what I'd said about wanting to reward Stephanie's trust. I had given her an absolutely insane story and she just... believed it. She needed to know she wasn't gullible or naïve. So I looked at the date one more time, closed my eyes, and went back.

Two hours later, I sat down across from Stephanie three minutes after I left. She already looked shocked, because I had come in from outside instead of returning from the bathroom. Luckily no one else in the restaurant seemed to have noticed. I took a drink of my ice water, which was still very cold despite how long I'd been gone.

"There was a basketball game," I said when I put down my water. "I couldn't tell you what position you were playing because I have no clue about the game, but you were wearing number 8. The uniforms were purple and white. I thought you were going to ask me the final score, so I was ready to watch the whole game, but about halfway through the first... uh, what? Quarter? Half?"

"Halves," she said quietly, still staring at me in shock. "College basketball has halves."

"Okay. Halfway through the first half, then. The ball went wild off the rim and hit a cheerleader in the face. It was *nasty*. Blood. And you ran over and cupped her face and held her until the medics could show up. When you got up, you kissed her on the lips. I figure something like that doesn't go over very well in a school with 'Our Lady' in its name."

Stephanie looked pale now. "No, it really doesn't."

I worried that I'd fucked up. Maybe she hadn't believed it after all and now she was going to run screaming from the restaurant.

"So~"

"It's true." She smiled, then shook her head. "That's crazy. I thought I believed you before, I truly did. But there's no way you could've figured that out so fast. You really went back there and saw it all happen, didn't you?"

I nodded.

She leaned forward again. "You were gone three minutes."

"Two hours. I just came back in a reasonable amount of time. I couldn't quite pop back into the exact place I left. And I wouldn't have wanted to, in case someone else had gone to the bathroom while I was gone. That could've been embarrassing."

"I'll bet." She took a drink of her water. "Her name was Nikki. We'd been dating in secret for about three months. When the basketball hit her, my heart stopped. And when I saw the blood, I-I forgot where I was and I just... I went to her. I barely even remember the kiss. But it got me kicked out of school. I told everyone that it wasn't reciprocated. I kissed her, she didn't kiss me. She was *furious* but I made her go along with the lie so she could stay in the school and not get in trouble."

"That's a pretty noble gesture."

She shrugged. "It was the right thing to do. I was the one who kissed her, and she'd already gotten smacked in the face by a basketball. She'd suffered enough."

I nodded. "So did you two...?"

"Dated for another six months or so, then things ended naturally." She shrugged. "We had a good run. She's a dentist now."

"Oh!" I nodded. "That's... uh, good for her. But what about you? I know more about your college ex-girlfriend than I do about you, and that's kind of weird."

She laughed. "It is weird. And for the record, I resent the fact I have to follow 'time traveler' when I say what I do for a living. There's no way I can live up to that."

"Well, time traveler isn't my job."

"Oh, no one pays you to go around and change history?"

"Not yet. I'm a chef."

She looked impressed. "I still think that's a little bit cooler than PE teacher."

I sat up straighter. "You're a PE teacher? Like, in a school?"

"Like in a school," she said. "Bachelder Middle School. I also coach the girls soccer team. They call me Coach Keith."

"That's so cool."

She grinned. "I feel like you'll have cooler stories, honestly. But I appreciate your enthusiasm." She tapped her menu and scanned the restaurant to make sure the waiter wasn't lurking. "Now that we've established you're not delusional and you won't be bored by me, maybe we should actually figure out what we're going to eat."

"Sounds like a plan."

I picked up my menu and realized I hadn't eaten anything yet today. I was suddenly ravenous. I wasn't too worried. If Stephanie could handle the reality of my time traveling, and if she was used to dealing with classes full of hormonal kids every day, she could handle seeing me destroy some chicken sate and a bowl of coconut soup.

CHAPTER THIRTEEN

The next morning, I slept a full hour past my alarm. Fortunately the restaurant didn't open until lunch, and I still had time to shower and get ready. "Time traveler running late," I muttered to myself as I finished brushing my teeth. "The irony." I got to work on time, if a bit out of breath, and did my job like it was any other day.

During a slow hour, I made a point to end up at the prep table next to Erin, my sous chef. "So," I said, striving to sound casual. "Have you ever heard of the FN Phantom...?"

She laughed. "Yeah, Chloe, I've listened to podcasts."

"There are podcasts?"

Erin stopped chopping. "Are you kidding? Basically every unsolved mystery true crime history of Chicago podcast out there has done an episode on her. How have *you* never heard of her?"

"Oh, you know how it is," I said. "It's almost like she didn't exist before yesterday."

"She definitely exists. Allegedly." She went back to chopping. "There are theories that it was all made up, the video footage was faked, and the staff just walked away with it.

But, like, where did the money go? Not one single bill ever showed up, in thirty years? Plus it was practically before the internet, even. They couldn't fake a video that well back then. Even if it was just cutting around her going in and out of the vault. How do you explain that?"

I shook my head. "I can't."

"What made you think of that?" Erin said.

"Oh, it just... you know, you go your whole life without hearing about something and then suddenly it's everywhere."

"I've had that. It's always super weird."

"Do you have any theories about who she might be?"

She shrugged. "I don't know. It happened in the eighties, right? She probably just ducked the two cameras they had in the hallway somehow, and then traded the money before computers could catch up with her. It's one of those things where people are trying to make it sound supernatural and mysterious when it's much more likely just sloppiness."

"Makes sense."

I finished my shift and went home. Ordinary day. Normal life. Not a bank robber, not an urban legend, not someone who had literally coughed up ashes from the Great Chicago Fire. I dropped onto the couch with the intention of closing my eyes for a few minutes to unwind from work. Instead I woke up when it was already dark outside, jerked out of a solid nap by the jingling of my phone. I turned it on, squinting at the intense light from the screen, and blinked a few times until the words came into focus.

A new message from Stephanie. I still didn't have a picture for her contact, but I'd assigned her name. I was immediately awake.

"Can you jump ahead three days?"

"In theory," I sent back. *"Why?"*

"Because I don't ask women out two days in a row. I figure three days is a good buffer."

I smiled. *"You would still be waiting, though."*

"You won't take me with you?"

I knew she was joking, but I honestly didn't know if it was

possible. Mom and I had jumped together, but we hadn't gone *together*. We just went to the same place at the same time. If I tried to take someone who didn't have the ability, would it work or just end messily?

"*I don't know if I can do that. Probably better to just be patient than risk tragedy.*"

"*You're probably right.*"

I sat up and ran my hand through my hair, still groggy. My phone jingled again and I looked at the screen to see another message from her.

"*So one thing you should know about me is that I suck at waiting. I'd rather break my rule and just ask you out again. Is it too late to meet for dinner?*"

It wasn't too late, and I hadn't eaten anyway. "*I just took a nap, so I can even stay up past my bedtime if I have to.*"

"*Wild woman. I'll do my best to keep up.*"

I replied, "*I chose last time, so I'll let you decide where we go tonight. You think, I'll get ready.*"

"*Sounds like a plan.*"

We said goodbye and I put the phone down. Texting had a lot of benefits to a phone call, but there was no equivalent to hanging up on a conversation. You both just stopped sending messages, but the conversation was just there. Open. Hanging. She could pop back any second with an "Oh one other thing…" Eventually I stopped drumming my fingers on the back of the phone and put it down on the cushion next to me.

A second date. It had been a long time since I had a second date with someone. I stood up and went to my closet to see if I had something to wear worthy of the honor.

***

She texted me an El station instead of an address. When I arrived, I found her waiting for me on a bench. She smiled when I appeared, slipping her phone into the pocket of her coat as she rose to meet me.

"I thought we could walk to the restaurant together."

"That's sweet. Lead the way."

We walked to the street together, and she gestured north. "So how was school today?" I laughed at the question before she could answer. "Sorry. That sounds so maternal."

Stephanie laughed. "I'm used to it by now. It was good. We played Jaws. It's this game where we put down these blue mats we have, and there are chairs and tables and things set up as islands and rocks. And the kids have to get to the safety of the bleachers without falling into shark-infested waters."

"That sounds amazing," I said. "All I remember from gym class is sit-ups and jumping jacks and running around the basketball court."

"We do that, too. But today I felt like being more fun." She bumped me with her elbow. "I must have been in a good mood or something."

I blushed. "Wouldn't know anything about that."

"It actually *is* great exercise. It's cardio disguised as a game. Plus it teaches them problem-solving and teamwork. Everybody wins."

"Except you, having to set up."

She waved that off. "Ah. I had my aide do it."

I laughed. "Clever."

"So... did you, um..." She held out her hand sideways and waved it side-to-side. "You know."

"Is that the signal for time travel?"

"I don't know, you're the expert."

I grinned and shook my head. "No. And no, I didn't. I went to work, actually. Long, hot, boring days making meals."

"I'm sorry if I'm obsessing over it," she said. "I know you're more than just... that."

"You can say the word," I said. "I understand. It's objectively interesting. It would be like if you went out with Buzz Aldrin and he got annoyed that you kept bringing up the Moon. You'll get bored of it eventually. And in the meantime, I don't have to worry about what to talk about over dinner. You're saving me the trouble of being interesting. I don't have shark-based cardio games to talk about, so I'm grateful for the built-in topic of conversation."

She said, "I just want to make sure you know I'm interested in you for more than that."

I blushed again. This woman was dangerous. "That's, um, nice information to have." I cleared my throat and scuffed my boot on the ground. "So is there anything you're particularly interested in knowing? Any burning questions?"

"I did think of a couple, yeah. Have you ever, you know, fast-forwarded? In a relationship, I mean. You're on a date, things are going well. You must be tempted to skip ahead to the morning to see if you've got a houseguest. Or, or maybe it's been a few weeks and you want to see what happens a year or two down the road."

I was already shaking my head. "Dangerous waters. I try not to go forward too often. I figured that out back in 2016, during the election."

She hissed through her teeth. "Ouch."

"The only thing worse than a nasty surprise is knowing it's on the way." I shuddered at the memory, the sinking sick feeling I'd had for the rest of the campaign season. "Especially with relationships. If you go forward and discover your partner cheated on you, then go back to *before* it happens, how do you decide what to do? You can't break up with someone for something they haven't done yet. But how can you stay with someone who would eventually do that? There's no way to win."

"I guess so," she said. "But it can save you from wasting time with a relationship that's doomed to fail."

"Maybe." I shrugged. "Not long ago, I went back in time and ran into an ex on the street. Except at that time, she wasn't an ex. We were still together, still happy. I had to make conversation with her. It was horrible."

"I'll bet."

"I could fast-forward and see how all my relationships will end. But then I would miss out on all the things that relationship taught me. No one starts out as the perfect partner. The rough bits get chipped away by all the bad relationships that came before until, eventually, you find someone with all the right rough bits chopped off of them, and you can make things work."

She smiled at me. "That's kind of beautiful. I almost feel

better about some of my past heartbreaks."

"Someone broke your heart?" I said. "Names and dates. I'll go back and kill them."

She laughed. "We'll save homicide until things are really going well."

"I guess that makes sense." I realized I hadn't seen any restaurants in half a block, and she seemed to be leading me into a residential area. "Where exactly are you taking me?"

"My place." Her eyes were almost apologetic. "I'm realizing now that's probably not the sort of thing you spring on somebody as a surprise. But I thought, you spend all day cooking for other people, you might appreciate someone going to the effort for you. I'm no chef, but I know my way around a kitchen well enough to feed two people."

I appreciated the thought, and the gesture, but more importantly I appreciated how nervous she seemed. She really wanted to impress me, and the effort she was going to made me feel special in a way I hadn't expected.

"If you prefer, there's a pizza place not far from here—"

"Something home-cooked sounds amazing right now," I interrupted. "Thank you for thinking of it."

She relaxed and sighed, nodded, and then pointed up the street. "We're not very far from my building. I went shopping after school, I had this recipe I printed out, and I thought, 'if she says no, I'll just make it anyway' and..." She stopped herself, took a deep breath, and let it out. "Sorry. I'm rambling and overexplaining. I tend to do that when I'm nervous. I haven't dated in a while."

"That's not a crime," I chuckled. "What do you have to be worried about?"

"Impressing you."

I moved closer to her. "You don't have to worry about that."

"Yeah?"

I nodded. "Yeah. You're doing better than you might think."

"Okay then." She smiled and pushed her shoulders up in

an almost-shrug, then pointed. "Well, now that we've taken care of that, let's go eat." We started across the street. "You can't judge my cooking, though."

"Oh, I'm going to judge. I'm a harsh critic. Gordon Ramsay tells me to take it down a notch."

"Maybe I'll poison your food."

"I'll just wait until I recover and come back to tonight and swap plates."

She shook her head. "Damn. Foiled again."

I laughed and followed her into the building. I wondered if it was normal for a second date to take place somewhere as intimate as one person's apartment. Was that a red flag? Or just a sign that she was, as she'd already confessed, out of practice at this sort of thing? I was just as inept, so I couldn't judge her. I decided to take the risk. I was enjoying my time with her enough that it was worth the risk of being poisoned to see where it went from here.

***

Dinner was Tuscan chicken with lemon. Not the most complicated dish in the world, but it showed she'd gone to the effort to take the extra step. I prepared to be effusive with my praise, but I was pleasantly surprised to discover I didn't have to exaggerate my enjoyment. It was fantastic, and I told her as much. She put on some music and, when we were finished eating, she settled back in her seat.

"I didn't think to get any dessert."

"I'm fine without dessert." Then, realizing no dessert meant that dinner might be coming to an end, I quickly added, "But... but, ah. There's music. We could dance."

She raised her eyebrows, then nodded. "I suppose we could dance, yeah."

We stood and moved to the empty space behind the couch. She was slightly taller so we made a silent agreement that she would lead. I wasn't entirely sure where to look. Putting my head on her shoulder seemed a little too intimate for a second date, but so did staring into her face. I settled for the latter just so my eyes wouldn't be darting all over the room, and she made the same decision.

We danced silently through the first verse of the current song before I saw something in her face change.

"Okay. I'm just going to ask you a question. And you're going to think I'm joking, or being glib, but it's a sincere question and I want you to answer it as such."

I nodded seriously. "I promise."

She took a deep breath and looked me in the eye. "Are you a demon?"

The corners of my mouth twitched, but I managed to stop myself from smiling. "What?"

"I know. It's ridiculous. It's superstitious and silly." She shook her head and closed her eyes. I noted her hands were still on my hips and we were still moving to the music. "But I grew up very religious. The Catholic girls school, you know. I don't even go to church anymore. But you literally appeared out of thin air in front of me. Coughing up smoke. Smelling like sulfur. You know things about me you shouldn't know. I just have to ask and get a sincere answer so I can shut up my stupid brain."

I allowed myself to smile. "No. I'm not a demon."

Stephanie rolled her eyes to the ceiling and let out a breath. "It's so stupid. But I'm actually a little relieved. Of *course* you're not a demon! It's insane."

"Not as insane as being a time traveler," I said. "But I like to think if I was a demon, I would've come up with a better lie than that. Something more believable so I could tempt you."

"Oh, so you're trying to tempt me now?"

I moved closer to her, pressing my hips against hers. "Why? Are you feeling tempted, Coach Keith?"

She let her eyes drift from my face, lower, tilting her head to one side before she raised them again. "Oh, I'm feeling all kinds of things, Chloe Cross."

"Interesting," I said. "Would it be out of line to kiss you?"

"Hm." She pretended to consider the question. "Second date, in my apartment, dancing. I don't think a kiss would be too far, no."

I smiled as I leaned in and pressed my lips to hers. I held

back a little, giving her the choice to make the kiss something more. Her tongue teased my lips apart. I slid my hands to the back of her neck, teasing the short hairs at the base of her skull as her fingers laced together in the small of my back. When I moved to change position, she pecked the corner of my mouth before starting a new kiss, a deeper kiss. Soon neither of us was paying any attention to the rhythm of the music; that wasn't what we were dancing to now.

Stephanie finally pulled back, flicking her tongue against my teeth once more for good measure before she opened her eyes. "Your breath doesn't taste like brimstone," she said. "That's a very good sign."

"And no forked tongue," I pointed out, extending it as evidence.

The thoughts that ran through her mind at that point were written plain as day all over her face. "Shame," she said. "That could've been... interesting."

I laughed and kissed her again. Stephanie took the lead again, moving me toward the wall between the living room and the kitchen. I was surprised but went willingly. She pinned me in place with her hips. Her kissing became more passionate, and I was suddenly very aware that I wouldn't be going home any time soon. I kept one hand in her hair but let the other move down to her waist. I found her belt loop and hooked two fingers in it, pulling her toward me.

Stephanie broke the kiss and rested her forehead against mine. "Since you asked permission before kissing me~"

"Yes," I interrupted.

She laughed. "I appreciate the enthusiasm." She pulled back and tossed her head to get her short bangs out of her eyes. "This is another serious question."

I cleared my throat and blinked a few times, furrowed my brow, doing an exaggerated impression of paying attention. She laughed again.

"Stop it."

"You're very serious," I said in a deep voice.

Stephanie said, "I am! Because it's important. Don't

tease."

I nodded. "Okay. Serious."

She took a deep breath. "I like to... be in control. And I can get a little rough. I'm not going to hurt you. And it's not the sort of thing where we need safe words. If you say stop, I stop. But when I see something I want, I-I... I take it."

"And you want me?" I asked quietly.

"Very much."

"Then take me."

Stephanie let out a shaky breath. She kissed me again, then grabbed the collar of my shirt and pulled me away from the wall. I was spun around, then she used her body to pin me again. I flattened my hands against the wall as she kissed my neck, moving her hands down the sides of my body. She traced my curves with her fingers and then moved up, lifting my shirt and letting her hands explore my stomach. I breathed in when she started fiddling with the button of my slacks. I arched my back, pressing my ass against her, and moved my hand down to guide her fingers inside once the button was undone.

Her hand slipped across the fabric of my underwear and she moved her lips back to my ear. "Do you like dirty talk?" she whispered.

"Yeah," I whispered back, then hissed when she started rubbing with two fingers.

"Do you like being called a good girl," she whispered, "or are you dirty?"

I thought for a second. "Is there a right~"

"Whichever gets you off," she said.

"Good girl," I said.

"Good girls still get spanked," she warned me.

My face felt like it was on fire. "I'm counting on it."

She pulled me away from the wall with her free hand on my shoulder, keeping the other between my legs as she guided me down the hall.

"Remember," she said, "if you say stop, I stop."

I had a feeling I wasn't going to be saying that particular

word that night.

***

"I don't normally do that on the second date."

I looked over at her. "Sex in general, or sex like *that?*"

"Either." She rolled onto her side and propped herself up on her elbow. "Was it okay?"

"It was intense for a first time," I admitted, chuckling. "And I would never classify it as 'okay,' just because I believe in being accurate in my rating systems. But if you're asking if it was too much or too far? Definitely not."

"Good..."

She put her hand on my hip and stroked my skin with two fingers. It gave me shivers, thinking about where those fingers had been not very long ago. The sex *had* been intense, more than I expected even after her disclaimer. She'd thrown me onto the bed and tore at my clothes, stopping just short of tearing or popping buttons. I almost told her it would be okay if she did rip something - I was far enough gone by that point that I wasn't even thinking about what I'd wear home - but she had my blouse undone before I could conjure the words.

Then it was a symphony of lips, tongue, and fingers in every possible combination. She teased me gently and then slapped my thigh, shocking a cry from me that turned into a moan as she kissed and sucked the stinging spot. She told me to ask what I wanted, demanded I tell her how she was making me feel, and she told me I was a good girl so many times that it started to feel like it was my own kink.

At one point she put her hand on my throat. When she applied pressure, I could feel my lips forming the word "stop," but she didn't go any further. I could live with the current level of her grip, the tightness of her fingers on my throat. It was strange, but it was also exhilarating. As long as she didn't squeeze any harder, it was fine. It was more than fine. It was kind of lovely, in fact. I put my hand lightly on her wrist and closed my eyes as she continued moving her other hand between my legs.

Stephanie took me to the edge and pulled me back so many times that I was close to screaming for orgasm by the time she finally took me there. My knees drew up, my fists pulled at her sheets, and I pressed down against her face with all the strength I could muster before I finally fell back and collapsed like a starfish in the center of her bed. But she didn't give me a chance to catch my breath. I was still dizzy from coming when she climbed up my body and straddled my face.

I'd lost all track of time, ironically. There was no way of telling how long she'd been edging me, and it's hard to keep track of minutes and seconds when someone as hot as Stephanie is squeezing your head between her thighs. It still felt early, though that could've just been my adrenaline working overtime. My heart still hadn't slowed down and the sweat hadn't even started drying on my body.

I reached out to trace her nipple, drawing a circle around it before I turned my wrist to take the whole breast in my palm. She giggled and arched her back into the caress.

"You like my little tits?" she said.

"I think they're perfect." I leaned closer and took her nipple into my mouth, gently sucking.

Stephanie sighed contentedly and kissed my hair, then started running her fingers through the strands.

"I decided it's okay if you're a demon," she said. "It's not a dealbreaker anymore."

I laughed and gently nipped at her nipple with my teeth. She yelped and gave me shoulder a gentle smack. "Bad girl."

I smiled and went back to sucking.

We might get to spanking after all.

CHAPTER FOURTEEN

We spent the next few days together. Sex, showering, running home long enough to get ready for work, then back to either her place or mine to start the process over again. Stephanie did enjoy things a little rougher than I was used to, but it was a nice change of pace. And it wasn't rough every single time. She could be tender and slow as well, and those times were so much sweeter than they otherwise would've been. Usually, between finishing and falling asleep, she asked whatever time travel questions she'd thought of since our last conversation.

"Can you take me back with you?"

"I don't know. I've never tried." We were in bed, cozy in her blankets. Her hand was resting on my stomach. I used the tip of my middle finger to draw an unbroken line up and down each of her fingers. "My clothes travel with me, thank goodness. And my phone and watch survive the trip. But I've never tried taking anything alive. And the idea of testing it on something... I mean, I don't want to risk killing something for an experiment. That's why I didn't become a brilliant scientist."

She said, "Oh, was *that* the reason."

"The one and only reason," I confirmed. "Where would you want to go if it was possible?"

Stephanie took a deep breath and considered the question. "It's hard to say. There are a lot of really good options. Could I stop an atrocity from happening?"

"Well, we talked about branching timelines, right? Other realities and always coming home to the world I recognize." Usually. "It's ultimately a good thing. I don't have to worry about the butterfly effect causing horrible consequences. But even if you could undo something awful, would you *physically* be able to do it? Like, everyone brings up killing baby Hitler. Like finding a particular baby in the middle of Germany or wherever he was born would be a snap."

"You make a good point. I wouldn't even know where to start looking for baby Hitler."

"Most hospitals have a Future Dictator maternity ward."

"Good to know. Okay. So I wouldn't even waste time trying to change the world. That's a huge weight off my shoulders."

I nodded. "Mine too."

"So something frivolous." She drummed her fingers on my stomach. "I would see Bowie live."

I groaned and closed my eyes. "Oh, I *knew* we were meant to be. That's always been a dream of mine, but I've never actually gone through with it. One of these days, though."

"You've been able to time travel your whole life and you never once used it to see Bowie?"

"It doesn't seem like the kind of experience you have alone."

She nodded. "I get that. Well, if you steal my idea, you have to tell me everything about it."

"I swear," I said. "And if I ever find out I can bring people along, you'll be my first passenger."

We sealed the promise with a kiss, and then a little more than a kiss. Stephanie never actually got a chance to ask her next question.

A few days later, while we were having dinner in her apartment, there was a knock on the door. She excused herself to go answer it, then returned looking ashen and shook. Before I could ask what was wrong, I noticed someone following her. It took me a second to realize it was another version of me.

"What's going on?" I asked the other me.

"Sorry." The other me was wearing a hoodie, hands in my pockets, looking sheepish. "I got here before she actually asked the question."

Color returned to Stephanie's face, pink flooding her cheeks. "I-I wasn't even sure I was going to bring it up."

"Apparently you did," I said, at the same time the other me said, "You will." I looked at myself. "Well, maybe now she doesn't have to."

Stephanie was hugging herself and trying very hard to avoid eye contact with either of us. "Oh boy." She looked at the new arrival. "I can't believe you actually showed up."

I put it together. "Oh! You wanted to have a threesome."

The other me smiled.

Stephanie put her hands over her face.

"I've always been a little curious," I admitted. "But you're really the first person who has ever gotten the whole story. So it's never been a real option before." I looked at me. "She brought it up, right? This wasn't our idea?"

"It would be a little conceited if it was *my* idea," the other me said.

I nodded. That was true.

"It was definitely my idea," Stephanie confessed. "I've been thinking about it for a while. I kept thinking it was too early to bring it up, or I was making excuses. I didn't want you to think I was weird or something. And maybe you'd think it was too weird to have sex with yourself~"

"I've had sex with myself a lot of times," both versions of me said.

Stephanie looked between us. "Really?"

I shrugged. "Given the opportunity, wouldn't you?"

She acknowledged that with a tilt of her head. "I suppose

so."

"That's a right answer," I said. "You're really hot."

"And good at sex," the other me added.

Stephanie laughed and pressed her hands against her cheeks. "Oh my god. This cannot be my reality."

The other me went to one of the unoccupied chairs at the table and sat down. "We can wait until you finish eating. I'm still full from dinner."

Stephanie had been returning to her seat but stopped. "Wait, you're from tonight...?"

The other Chloe nodded. "We finished eating and then I popped back. I misjudged the time."

I shook my head knowingly. "Short hops are always the worst."

"You try for an hour, you get twenty minutes~"

"Try for twenty minutes and you get six hours."

"I overshot the landing, too. I was about a mile away and had to hurry. I guess I hurried too much. I just didn't want to get here after I'd already jumped back and~"

I shuddered at the thought. "A never-ending loop."

"What a nightmare."

Stephanie had been watching our back-and-forth like a tennis match. "Do you two even need me?"

We both looked at her. I smiled and said, "We'll find a use for you."

Other Chloe smiled mischievously.

***

I don't recommend having two threesomes in the same night. Even if they're with the same people. It's just unnecessarily exhausting.

When we finished the first time, which I thought was great, I realized we were in a situation where there were two versions of me in the same time period. So in order to preserve the loop, I kissed Stephanie goodbye, kissed myself because Stephanie really liked watching that, and got dressed. I went back in time to earlier in the evening and came back to the apartment. This time, I was the early and unexpected arrival.

After the second go-around, when the other version of me left to continue the loop, Stephanie watched the door for a long time. Then she let her eyes travel up and down my body as if trying to memorize my curves.

"So..." She furrowed her brow. "I feel like you're... new. Like the person I've been dating just left, and I'm never going to see her again. And you're the replacement. But you *are* her. Right?"

I nodded. "By your logic, I left the Stephanie *I've* been dating when I traveled back. But it's still you. And I'm still me. I'm just a few hours older."

"And you've lived this night twice."

"Right."

She dropped her head onto the pillow. "This is insane."

I put my head down next to hers. "Try living it."

Stephanie rolled onto her side to face me. "How have your other partners dealt with it?"

"It's never come up."

"How could it *possibly* have never–" Realization dawned in her eyes. "Oh. You were telling the truth. I really am the first person you've ever trusted with the secret."

"You are. It's never been worth the trouble of trying to explain all this before."

Stephanie raised her eyebrows, then looked over the top of my head. She had a strange look on her face, like she was trying not to smile. She put her hand on my hip and stroked her fingers up and down slowly.

"I'm, um. I'm honored. That's a lot of pressure to put on–"

"I know," I said. "Trust me, I know. We've only been together for a week or so. But I think I just proved beyond a shadow of a doubt that time works differently for me. I have a good feeling about you. This. Us. I don't want to scare you or put any pressure on you to meet my speed. I'm only being honest."

"I appreciate that." She looked me in the eye again. "And I feel that bond with you, too. Enough that I... I'm going to tell you something that I normally reserve for... well, much later in the relationship."

My mind flooded with possibilities, a surge of fear and excitement. Nothing good ever followed a prologue like that, but knowing she was about to share something intimate was weirdly exciting. I'd just had sex with the woman twice (technically four times) in the same night but this was a whole different kind of closeness.

"I was married. To a man. When I was nineteen. It only lasted three years. But it was long enough to get pregnant."

I blinked in surprise. "You had a... you have a kid?"

"A daughter." She smiled, but it was a sad smile.

"Did something happen to her?"

"No," she said, confused. "She's fine. She's studying literature at Northwestern."

I pushed myself up on one elbow. "Wait. She's in college."

"You heard me say 'nineteen,' right?" She rolled onto her back. "How old do you think I am?"

"No, it's not..." I sighed and pushed my hair out of my face. "I knew that you were older than me. You told me you were in college in 2002. So I just would've had to do the math on that. And I would've, if it bothered me. But I don't care that you're... forty-two?"

She chuckled. "Forty-four. I appreciate the skim."

"Right. There's knowing *that* and comparing it with the idea that you're technically old enough to have a kid who is in college studying literature right now."

"She's twenty-three, if that helps the math."

"Wow," I muttered. After a few seconds, I realized how my reaction must have seemed to her. I put my hand on her thigh. "This isn't about you. Not really. I don't care about the fact you're older than me. Well. Okay. Technically I guess I *do* care, but I consider it a perk. This is about the fact you... you have a *child*. A person out there in the world. And I'm..." I sighed. "Me, I've just been out here fucking around. Work, time travel, sleep with someone, work, time travel..."

"Visit the Great Chicago Fire."

I chuckled. "Yeah. I just feel very unaccomplished next to you. That's all."

She sat up and kissed my shoulder, then my neck. "You're the most interesting person I've ever met, Chloe Cross."

"Thank you, Stephanie Keith." I turned my head and kissed her lips. "What's your daughter's name?"

"Jessica."

"Jessica Keith," I thought. "Pretty name."

She smiled and kissed me again. "You're not freaked out?"

"Unless she's here, in the other room."

Stephanie laughed. "No, no, she lives in Evanston. But I wanted you to know because the past few days, when I haven't been freaking out because *oh my god, my girlfriend is a time traveler*, I've been thinking about if and when I want you to meet her. That's not a conversation I take lightly."

"No, I'm sure," I said. "And I take it as the honor it is."

I lowered myself again and she came with me, resting her head on my shoulder. "I still don't know when it will happen. But I'm more and more convinced that it will. So I wanted you to be prepared for it, too."

"I'll start preparing," I promised her.

"Good." She kissed my chest. "Get some sleep. You've had a busy night."

I grinned. "It's not work if you love your job."

She laughed and pinched me.

I settled in and closed my eyes, but I kept thinking about her confession. A daughter. An adult daughter, who could drink and vote and everything.

"Whenever you're ready," I said quietly, "I'd love to meet your daughter."

And honestly, if I could go back and erase *anything* I've *ever* said, I wouldn't even have to think about it before choosing that sentence.

Chapter Fifteen

We had been together for just over a month when Stephanie called to let me know Jessica was coming for a visit. "Very low-key. Just mom-daughter time. But if you want to come over and have dinner with us one night while she's here... She knows I'm dating someone. I've told her we don't know how serious it is yet..."

"We don't?" I was leaning against the brick wall in the alley outside the kitchen door. It was a little enclosed nook that started as a smoking spot, then became nothing, and now had evolved into a place for the staff to vape.

She chuckled. "Well, we haven't had the conversation. But she knows that it's enough to include meeting the family."

"That works for me," I said, smiling. "And I won't be offended if she decides to pass. It's a lot to ask, and she probably just wants to spend time with you. We'll play it by ear."

Jessica was in town for four days, and we all eventually agreed that I would cook them dinner on Saturday night at my apartment. I spent the night before planning the menu, and the next morning scoured farmer's markets looking for only the best ingredients. I only texted Stephanie twice, maybe five times, about any dietary restrictions or preferences her daughter might have. I was just trying to be a good hostess. I didn't care about Jessica's judgement. I didn't need her approval. I just wanted her to be aware that her mother could be with a gourmet chef that could make mouth-watering dishes whenever she desired.

I spent the afternoon making the dinner. It wasn't anything particularly fancy, just bruschetta chicken with grilled potatoes and asparagus.

Okay, maybe I needed her approval a little bit. Sue me.

Stephanie texted when they were on their way. I had a brief panic attack because I hadn't planned what I was wearing. I suddenly felt like an adult. I hated feeling like an adult. I was still figuring shit out, I was dating, I was young and hot and desirable, and suddenly I was on the "mom" side of the table. How dare Stephanie just spring this on me?

I decided it was best not to overthink the outfit. Black slacks, red blouse. Don't go overboard. Look nice, but don't put on a damn costume.

They arrived right on time. I kissed Stephanie on the cheek, then turned to face her daughter. Jessica was holding a paper bag, presumably the ice cream cake Stephanie had promised to bring for dessert. I was shocked by the sight of her. Jessica looked much more like an adult than I was ready for. She was a fully grown human, like a bank teller or a barista, and looking at her made me feel like a senior citizen. But I managed a smile and awkwardly held out my hand to her.

Stephanie looked at my hand, then looked at Jessica. She took the cake from her and stepped aside. "Jessica, this is Chloe. Chloe... meet my daughter."

Jessica smiled. "Hi, Chloe. Mom's told me a lot about you already." She looked at my hand, which I only then realized I hadn't lowered, and gave me a perfunctory shake. "You have a lovely place."

"Thanks," I said. "I'm a chef."

"I can tell," Jessica said. "I spent the whole walk down the hall hoping that smell was coming from your apartment."

I closed the door behind them and took Stephanie's coat. I hung it on a hook and, when I turned, I caught Jessica staring at me. She looked away quickly, pretending she had just been examining the wall art. A couple of framed prints I'd put up mainly so the living room wouldn't look quite so empty. I cleared my throat and tried not to feel self-conscious as I guided them to the dinner table.

"Dinner just needs to be served up," I said. "Have a seat and I'll bring everything out."

"I'll help you," Stephanie said.

Jessica held up her hands. "Actually, if I could wash up...?"

"Sure," I said, pointing her toward the bathroom.

When she was gone, Stephanie said, "Oh my god, she despises you."

My stomach dropped into my shoes. "*What?*"

Stephanie laughed. "I'm kidding. I'm just kidding." She put her hands on my shoulders and kissed me. "I'm sorry. I thought it would be funny. She... well, she couldn't have formed an opinion yet, but she really did say something about the smell in the hallway. You're starting off strong. Just relax and be yourself, okay? You'll do fine."

I tried to unwind myself from the knots I'd worked myself into. "Okay. I'll relax. It'll be fine. She's your kid, right? She's like you."

Stephanie made a face. "Well..."

"Just agree with me," I pleaded.

"Okay," Stephanie laughed, kissing me again. "Yes, she is exactly like me. We have the same tastes and we like everything the same."

"Good." I hugged her, then stepped back and led her into the kitchen.

Conversation started off a little rocky. I didn't want to sound like a corny sitcom girlfriend, trying to ingratiate myself to a kid. But every other attempt I made to speak with her made me feel like I was doing a job interview. Stephanie was marvelous at playing intermediary. She suggested topics, pointed out areas of interest we had in common, and tried to keep us both engaged.

Jessica did her part, asking me questions and answering whatever lame softballs I lobbed her way. But when Stephanie was talking, or when there was a lull, I noticed that she kept looking at me like I had something on my face. I managed to stop from wiping my cheeks or nose, but I swept my tongue over my teeth a few times just to make sure nothing was stuck there.

Toward the end of the main course, Jessica finally held up her hands. "I'm sorry. I've been trying to figure this out all night. You look *so* familiar to me. Have we met before?"

Dread clutched my heart. "Um, no," I said. "I don't think so."

"I swear I've seen you somewhere before. It's just at the edge of my mind. Like if I glance at you, for a split second it'll be right there..." She gripped her chin like a cartoon version of Sherlock Holmes and squinted at me. "So weird. It's going to drive me nuts. You know how you'll have a memory of something, and you remember the things *around* the thing...? Like, 'I saw this once, and it was inside a box and I was outside,' something like that. That's how I feel when I look at you."

"Like I was in a box outside?"

She shook her head. "No, that was just an example."

"Well, as far as I know, I've never been to Northwestern," I said.

Jessica said, "Well, I lived here with Mom before I started going there. Maybe we ran into each other at... Macy's? No, that's not it." She shook her hands with frustration. "God! It's going to make me insane!"

I cleared my throat and pushed my chair back. "You can think about it while your mom and I clear up the dishes and things. Are we doing dessert?"

"Absolutely," Stephanie said.

We took the dishes into the kitchen. As soon as we were

alone, Stephanie leaned close enough that I could feel her breath on my cheek.

"Is there a chance you *will* meet her before tonight?" she whispered.

I sighed. "You're already pretty good at this. Yeah, there's a chance I'll eventually go back in time and our paths will cross before tonight. But I know what she looks like. I think I would avoid that sort of thing from happening."

"Maybe that's why you stuck in her mind." Stephanie looked over her shoulder to make sure Jessica hadn't followed us into the room. "Maybe she was out for a walk in the park and she saw some crazy woman who suddenly changed direction and ducked into a bush to avoid being seen. That would explain why she can't pin you down."

I got out plates and a knife to cut the cake. "This doesn't have to be a disaster," I said. "We can just write it off as mistaken identity. I've done it before."

"This happens a lot?"

"More than you might think. Chicago can be a really small town sometimes. It's ridiculously inconvenient."

I cut the slices and Stephanie got the silverware.

When we took the plates back out, I looked at Jessica with fake hope. "Any luck?"

"No. I'm really starting to worry I made an idiot out of myself for no reason."

I laughed. "Mistaken identity. Happens all the time."

"You could have just crossed paths at some point," Stephanie suggested. "Chicago can be a really small town sometimes."

I looked at her and tried not to smile at the fact she'd stolen my line. She hid her own smile behind her fork, covering it up with a bite of cake.

"Sorry," Jessica said. "If it hasn't come to me yet, it's not going to magically snap into place."

"Let me know if it winds up being a celebrity," I said. "I can always use an ego boost. Unless it's that arrow guy from the Avengers movies."

Jessica said, "Hey, Jeremy Renner is hot."

Stephanie waved her fork at me. "I forgot to warn you. Jessica is straight."

"Well, we all have flaws." I winked at Jessica and took a bite of my cake.

***

I dropped onto the couch after they left. Jessica had gone ahead to the stairs so her mother and I could say goodbye privately. Stephanie held the lapels of my blouse, kissed me, and then whispered against my lips. "She likes you. She relaxed, she laughed a lot, she liked you."

"Let me know what she says on the way home," I whispered back.

Stephanie winked. "I'll give you a full progress report. Bye."

"Goodnight," I said, stepping away from her. I watched them go, then went inside and cleaned up the remnants of our meal and started the dishwasher.

I stared at the ceiling and tried not to think about Jessica recognizing me. It hadn't been ideal, of course, but it seemed like we'd managed to overcome the hurdle with ease. People recognized other people all the time. Nothing weird or supernatural about it. No reason to make a huge fuss. And I agreed with Stephanie's assessment that the night had gone well. Jessica had seemed relaxed and casual by the end of the night. She even mocked my stiff-armed handshake when I saw them out. I think it's a very positive sign if she's comfortable enough to make fun of me.

I was about to get up and start getting ready for bed when there was a knock on the door. I checked the time and frowned. I had turned out the overheads, so the only light in the room was bleeding through from the kitchen. It suddenly set a very ominous mood and I wanted very much to turn on every light in the apartment before I investigated the mysterious knock.

"Who is it?"

"Jessica. Keith."

I frowned and got up. I checked the peephole to confirm

it was her, then opened the door. "Hi. Did you forget something?"

"No." She looked anxious. "I need to talk with you. Can I come in?"

"Sure." I stepped back and let her in. "What's going on? Is your mom okay?"

Jessica nodded. "Yeah. She's home. I told her I had to run to the store and grab something real quick. I didn't want to tell her I was coming back here."

"Why not? What's wrong?"

"I remembered where I know you from."

Her words were like a smack in the middle of my chest. My knees were rubbery, but I managed to keep them locked so I wouldn't topple backward. I crossed my arms over my chest, bracing myself for the worst. And considering that she and I may have history that happened in my future, I felt justified in being afraid. She had been looking down at her feet, almost like she was embarrassed. Oh, god, what had I done to this girl?

God, what had I done *with* this girl...? Please don't be that. Please.

She took her phone out and turned on the screen. I held my breath as she swiped away the lock screen and turned the phone around so I could see what she'd looked up.

My legs threatened to fail me again.

"Do you know anything about the FN Phantom?"

CHAPTER SIXTEEN

I stared at the thirty-year-old sketch artist version of my face. I slowly looked up at Jessica, who was swaying awkwardly and chewing on her thumbnail. I raised my eyebrows at her.

"Okay." I didn't want to give her any ammunition until I knew exactly what she was accusing me of. "I've seen that image before."

"Everyone has," she said, lowering her phone. "Anyone who has ever looked up the Phantom online, anyway. See, a couple of years ago, there was this podcast covering unsolved mysteries, and they did a whole five part series on the story. It made me curious enough that I looked stuff up online. That picture is on the Wiki and most of the Google searches. That's why I couldn't place you. It was so out of context that I couldn't put the pieces together until I got home and went to check my mail."

"So..." I still didn't want to connect any dots for her.

"Look, I know we just met. This is a really huge thing to drop on a relative stranger. But is there any chance your mother was the Phantom?"

I could breathe again. It seemed ridiculous now for her to

make the leap to time travel.

"You think my mother stole... how much was it? A quarter of a million dollars?" I laughed. "Honey, when I was a kid, McDonald's was a luxury. If Mom had that kind of cash stashed away, I would've known about it."

"Maybe she has it stashed away for an inheritance. It would explain why none of it ever showed up! If she took it for you and kept it hidden until she passed away--"

"Then I would've gotten it when I was ten," I said, regretting how harsh the words came out when Jessica flinched hard. "I'm sorry. But my mother..." I realized that this had only been a fact of my life for a few weeks. All the timelines crashing together meant that I was living in the world where I wasn't abandoned on a bench. Maybe that's why things were going so well with Stephanie when all my past relationships had been utter disasters.

"You don't have to explain," Jessica said. "I'm sorry I brought it up."

I shook my head. "Don't be. That picture really *does* look a lot like me. You know who I *don't* resemble, though? My mother. She's Chinese, but I'm part English thanks to my father. Her face is thinner than mine, she has fuller lips... No one would ever describe her to a sketch artist and get that result. So unless you think I'm a really well-preserved seventy..."

She laughed, embarrassed now. "No, I know you're not *that* old."

"You didn't have to quantify it, you know. You could've just said not old. That would've been... just fine."

She chuckled again. "Sorry." She cleared her throat and shuffled her feet nervously. "I should go. I've wasted enough of your time. And Mom is going to start wondering where I am. Could you, um, not mention this to her? I think she was already weirded out by the fact I recognized you from somewhere. And now that I have the answer, even if it's not really you, I can let it go."

I nodded. "Mum's the word. Or, uh... you know."

"Right." She stepped forward and I moved out of the way. I opened the door for her. "My dad *was* D.B. Cooper, though."

She laughed. "Family tradition, I guess. Let me know if you find a couple hundred thousand dollars in your mom's jewelry box sometime."

"Will do."

I closed the door on her, then sagged against it with my head to the wood. "Fuck," I whispered. "Fuck, damn, shit." I turned around and rested my back against the door. After taking a minute to collect my thoughts, I took out my phone and dialed Stephanie.

She answered quickly. "Hey. If you're looking for phone sex, we have to be quick. Jess is at the store but I don't know when she'll be back."

I smiled, tempted in spite of the circumstances. "I'll take a raincheck. You know I like to take my time with you." Even her laugh was seductive. "Listen, we need to talk. Not right now, not tonight. But maybe after Jessica goes home. Tomorrow, right?"

"Yeah." Her voice was immediately more serious. "What's going on? Is everything okay?"

"Everything's fine." I started to pace. "Jessica figured out where she recognizes me from."

There was a sharp intake of breath on her end. "Wait, how do you- wait, did she go back to your place after we left?"

"It's fine," I said. "She didn't want me to tell you, so I don't think she's going to bring it up. But it's something you should know about."

"Does it involve time traveling?"

"Yeah," I said.

Stephanie breathed out. "Okay. I'll brace myself. Jessica is leaving after lunch tomorrow. We can meet up... where? When?"

"I'm at work until dinner," I said. "Meet me there at five, and we can come back here."

"That works. Chloe... how bad is it?"

"Probably not great," I admitted. "Nowhere near as bad as

it could be. I think it depends on your morality levels."

She laughed without humor. "Okay. Wow. That was not the answer I expected. Just..." She made a gagging, grunting sound. "Tell me you didn't sleep with her."

"No," I said firmly. "Absolutely not."

Stephanie let out a relieved sigh. "Then I think I can deal with whatever it actually is."

"I hope so. I'll see you tomorrow."

"See you then."

I hung up and sat down on the couch. I pressed the phone to my forehead and closed my eyes. The Jessica situation could have gone better, but it wasn't a disaster. We'd hit it off pretty well, in fact. It felt like a success, since I've managed to not be outed as a bank robber. But I'd put out that fire... no joke intended... and she seemed to sincerely believe my story. The sketch was just a weird coincidence. It was the only explanation that made sense.

Once that was out of my mind, I focused on the fact that Stephanie and I had both sincerely worried that, at some point in time, I'd slept with her daughter. The fact we'd both considered it a possibility wasn't a great testimony to my character. Whoever my character was now, after all these timelines started crashing into each other, changing my past and affecting me in ways I didn't realize until words came crashing out of my mouth. Would it eventually settle down? Or was I just doomed to keep subtly shifting under the surface?

"Fuck, did I fuck up the entire universe?" I rubbed my hands over my face.

Maybe I should just stop time traveling altogether. It was fun revisiting memories, and I really did like fucking myself once in a while, but it only seemed to fuck things up in the long run. I was with Stephanie now. Stephanie was nice, she was lovely, she was funny and cool, and it might be nice to settle down a little. I'd done enough damage. The smart thing to do would be to retire from the hobby before I ruined anything else.

***

And since we still haven't gotten to Darwin, I think it's obvious I didn't take my own very good advice. No need to point it out to me. We're getting to him very soon, I promise.

***

The next afternoon, Stephanie arrived at Trilogy fifteen minutes before the end of my shift. I went out to ask if she wanted a snack while she waited, which she passed on, but she ordered an iced tea. I delivered it myself and she let her fingers brush my hand when I gave it to her. She ran her eyes up and down my body, examining my checkered pants and white chef's jacket. She looked up at my hair.

"Do you have one of the hats with the cute name?"

"Toque," I said. "And yes."

"I'd like to see you in it sometime."

I grinned. "Play your cards right. I won't be too long."

She nodded and told me to take my time. When I got back to the kitchen, Erin smiled and raised her eyebrows at me.

"Is that your *girlfriend?*" she asked, drawing the word out as much as possible.

I said, "Don't be a child. I'm an adult, a fact that was painfully brought to my attention last night. She has a daughter in college."

Erin craned her neck to look out in the dining room again. "So? She's about the right age."

"No, she's not!" I said, slapping Erin's arm with the back of my hand. She is around my age, and I'm still youthful and vibrant."

Erin said, "Oh honey."

"Shut up! I'm thirty-three!" Ish.

She laughed and went back to her station. "If you have plans with her, you can skip out a little early. You've covered for me plenty of times, I wouldn't mind."

"Are you sure?"

She shrugged and then nodded. "We're all right at the moment. Unless we get a bus from a senior citizens center looking for the early bird special, I can fly solo for fifteen minutes." She put a hand over her mouth. "Oh, sorry. I didn't mean to say 'senior citizen.' Did I trigger you?"

"I'm going to sauté your head. But thanks, Erin. I appreciate it."

"Sure. You grandmas gotta get home early so you can be in bed by sundown."

I said, "Keep it up, smart ass. Hope you like sixteen hour shifts and working Christmas."

"We're not even open on Christmas."

"You could clean everything," I suggested. "The place would be sparkling!"

I cleaned up my station and headed back out to let Stephanie know we could leave early. She finished her tea and followed me outside.

"So how worried should I be?" she asked when we were on the sidewalk. "The moral compass qualifier has really been messing with my head all day. Did you kill someone?"

"No," I said. "It's actually connected to the day we met."

She frowned. "When you came back from the Great Chicago Fire?"

I nodded. I hooked my arm around hers and started walking, guiding her north toward the river. "I didn't just go there on a whim, or to see history being made. There was something I had to do."

"In 1880-whatever?"

"Right. Do you know about the FN Phantom?"

Stephanie said, "The bank robber? Of course. She walked into a vault, they shut the door, and then she…"

Stephanie stopped walking. I tried to pull her along for a few steps, but my arm just slipped away from hers. I turned around to face her. She was staring at me, jaw dropped, eyes wide.

"It's *you?*" She looked around at the other people on the sidewalk, who were thankfully ignoring us. She moved closer and lowered her voice. "First you tell me that you can… do what you do. And now you're telling me you're also one of Chicago's most infamous criminals?"

"I don't know about *most* infamous," I muttered. "We had actual mob bosses running the town for a while..."

"That's not the point!" She pushed both hands into her hair. "She... *you*... stole a million dollars!"

"A quarter of–" I shook my head. "Never mind. Not important."

Her eyes widened even more. "*Not important?* In today's money that would be, like... it would..." She gave up. "Over twice as much."

"Yeah. It's not like I still have it."

"You robbed a bank," she hissed.

"Thirty years ago."

She narrowed her eyes. "*Technically.* But it wasn't thirty years ago to *you*, was it. Do you think that makes it better?"

"Kind of. But I don't know why."

Stephanie walked away from me and crossed her arms. I let her put the space between us, worried by the way she kept working her jaw. I was very aware of the fact we were on the street with people moving around us like we were rocks in a stream. They kept their eyes forward, their attention on their phones or their companion. None of them were paying attention to what was happening with me and Stephanie, but they were all aware. I felt awkward being so on display, so I finally moved closer to her.

"Maybe we can talk about this at my apartment."

"No," she said, turning to face me. "I don't know what I think yet. But I'm pretty sure nothing you say will help me figure it out. It'll just confuse me. So I'm going to go home and I'll think about it there. And then I'll probably call you and *then* we can talk. Or..."

I flinched. "Or?"

She shook her head and sighed. "I don't know, Chloe. You understand this is a lot, right? This is a big fucking deal. And it's not a hypothetical game I've ever played. Like... like, would I stay with someone if they cheated on me. The answer to that one is a hard *no*, by the way."

"It's the right answer."

"Just so we're clear on that."

"Same page." I risked touching her arm. "But we're... we're going to be okay, right?"

She looked me in the eye. "Honestly, Chloe? If I have to answer right now, the best I can give you is an 'I don't know.' I hope we are. But..." She shook her head and stepped away from me again. "If I decide this is a dealbreaker, what's stopping you from just going back and stopping yourself from telling me?"

I had thought the same thing. "My word?" I shrugged. "That's all I have. It would be the same as cheating, really. If I knew you would end our relationship over something I did, and I kept that from you, it would be the same as if I slept with someone else. I wouldn't do that."

She seemed to relax. Just a little.

"Okay. I still need... I just need to think."

I watched her walk away and tried to come up with a more ominous word than "think" when it came to relationship.

CHAPTER SEVENTEEN

I stood across the street and watched the building. It was familiar to me now, the memories of it buried deep in my brain like old photographs at the back of a drawer. Even though they were brand new, even though they had only existed since the whole bank robbery fiasco. I knew which window was my childhood bedroom, and I watched it until I saw the light go on. I checked my watch to confirm the time, then crossed the street. I used the hide-a-key to let myself into the apartment.

In the kitchen, I found a pint of Blue Bell ice cream. I knew which drawer the silverware was in, went to it without even thinking, and took a seat at the dinner table. I could hear voices down the hall - idle conversation and laughter - and I tried not to feel jealous of it. This night had happened to me. If I tried, if I focused, I could probably remember it.

The pint was half gone when I heard the goodnights. A few seconds later, Mom came down the hall. She looked exhausted, but in that grateful way all mothers had. She started for the couch, then sensed she wasn't alone and turned to look at me. I took another bite while she processed my presence, then she came to join me.

"That's your ice cream. Just so you know."

"And I waited over twenty years to eat it," I said. "You should be impressed by my self-control."

She shushed me and hooked her thumb toward the back of the apartment. "She just fell asleep."

"She's a heavy sleeper at this age." I looked around the kitchen, then gestured vaguely with my spoon. "I remember this place, by the way. Which is strange, because I never lived here. At this age, I was with John and Denise Howser. They were nice. Nowhere near ready to be a forever home, but definitely an A for effort. Anyway, I remember them, but I also knew this is where we lived after everything changed. I even know what my bedroom looks like. Isn't that fucked up?"

"Watch the language."

I muttered an apology and scraped my spoon along the edge of the carton. Mom rested her chin on her hand, waiting for me to finish rambling and get to the point.

"I want to erase the FN Phantom."

She sighed. "Chloe..."

"I know we can't undo the actual bank robbery. Apparently. But there has to be a way we can stop it from becoming a whole stupid phenomenon. Thirty years later and everyone knows that police sketch. Everyone knows the story. They did an SNL sketch about it! Courteney Cox played me. That was pretty cool, I guess."

"I don't know her."

"*Friends?*"

She shook her head.

"Maybe it hasn't premiered yet. That's not the point. I don't want this thing haunting me. We've basically already erased it. The money is gone. I just want to lose the mystery, too."

"There are bound to be consequences. You've screwed up the timeline enough. So many timelines collapsed into each other. Like you said, you remember this apartment even though you never lived here. And if you ever went and visited the Howser people, people you remember as foster parents, they wouldn't know who you are. Because it didn't happen to them. You're not the only person affected by the collapsing, Chloe. For most people, they can write it off as a bad memory or a think they're remembering a weird dream. But other people won't be able to cope. Their reality will seem off and nothing will ever make it right."

"And that's my fault."

She started to say something comforting, then shrugged. "Yes. This time, it was because of you."

"I should just go back. Stop myself from meeting you at the hospital. That's where this whole mess started."

"Oh good. Create another timeline. That will fix things."

"If timelines can collapse, let's just get rid of this one! It seems pretty shitty all around anyway. I'm doomed to forever wonder if I'll be outed as a bank robber. My girlfriend is probably going to dump me because of it."

Mom sat up straighter. "Wait, what?"

I shook my head and waved her away. "Never mind. I don't mean it." I sighed and slumped forward. "It would probably cause a hundred other problems. And it wouldn't fix things with Stephanie, it would just take away her knowledge of what I did. And that's... sort of like lying?" I narrowed my eyes. "Lie of omission, maybe...?"

"You're trying to keep the truth from her so she can't make an informed decision. That's lying."

"Right. So I don't want to do that."

"Good. If it's any consolation, I'm glad I met you that day in the hospital. I'm glad you convinced me to stick around."

I was depressed and feeling 'fuck-it' enough to ask something I'd always been afraid to have answered. "Why *did* you abandon me? I mean. You seem like a decent enough person. Is it because my father wasn't around? Oh, by the way? My father? Never knew anything about him, and then the other night, out of nowhere, I told someone he was English. And my brain just kind of said, 'oh yeah, English, died before I was born, you've known that since grade school.' I hate that. I *hate* that."

She twisted her lips and looked down at her hands. "The reason... is a very long story."

I glared at me. "We have time."

Mom laughed. "I suppose we do." She sighed and leaned back in her seat. "God. Okay. Well, first, I have to tell you that we're not the only time travelers. But we might be the last."

I actually got chills. "Okay."

"There were never very many. And they were good at finding each other. Usually five, never more than nine. They would pop into the future and check on sporting events, stocks, horse races. Anything they could bet on. Then they'd come back and make a fortune gambling. They kept their heads down otherwise. Just gambled and built their wealth, and started families to pass on the time travel gene. Then, one generation of kids came along, and not one of them could do it. The old men got desperate and became very focused on continuing the line. I won't horrify you with all those details—"

"Thanks."

"But they did everything in their power to make sure time traveling continued. A group of seven turned into five, then three. Eventually, there were just two. Me. And your father."

I looked over my shoulder at the fridge. "Am I going to need alcohol for this part?"

She smiled sadly. "No. We really were in love. We were planning to get married eventually, after you were born. Neither of us thought you'd have the ability. We were so damn certain of it."

"So what happened?"

"Well, you're not the only one with two memories. What really happened, in this version of reality, is that you walked into my hospital room as a full-grown adult the same day I'd given birth to you. And that's how this version of me figured it out. But I also remember a reality where I time traveled a few years into the future to see for myself. I had to know for sure."

She was quiet for so long that I had to prompt her. "And?"

"I found the future version of myself. You were gone. While your father and I were the final time travelers, the children of the others lived on. The failures born without the ability." There were tears in her eyes. "They were bitter, naturally. And they hated that they couldn't continue milking their father's cash cow. So when they found out I'd given birth, they... they came and took you. They wanted to find out how you could do what you do. By any means necessary."

"Oh my God."

She breathed in deep and nodded, staring at an empty spot on the table. "So I left you on a park bench and got the hell out of there. They eventually showed up, but I lied. Told them you were stillborn. They didn't believe me at first but, after a lot of digging, they accepted I wasn't hiding you. And only a monster would abandon a newborn, right? So they left me alone."

"Where was my father during all of this?"

This time her tears actually did fall. "He died a few months into the pregnancy. Nothing nefarious. Just an accident. And then I was the last person who could travel in time. Until.." She held her hands out toward me.

"So what happened this time? Did they just give up?"

Mom shook her head. "No, they came. They were determined to take you with them."

"What did you do?"

She reached for the ice cream. I let her steal it and the spoon, waited for her to take a bite. "They're gone."

"You... did you...?" I found the word. "Kill them?"

She shook her head. "No..."

"That was a *weirdly* soft 'no,' Mom."

She said, "I didn't kill anyone. I knew who they were and when they would come for me, from the previous version of events. So I went to them first. One by one. I introduced myself. I asked them if they wanted to know what it was like to time travel. 'More than anything.' They all said that, the exact same way. More than anything. So. I showed them."

I remembered Stephanie asking if I could take her with me when I traveled. "You can do that? Take someone else with you?"

She nodded. "To be honest, I wasn't sure the first time. No one had ever been willing to test it on a living subject. But it worked. I held his hands and took him away."

I blinked at her. "How... how far..."

"There's a trick to it," she said. "Because men have a tendency to... multiply, you know? And if you just drop a man in the middle of a new time period, there's always a chance that in a few years, there will be new children being born, and then you have a population boom, and it's a..." She waved her hand. "It's a whole thing. Going back too far, you risk creating a whole population. Not to mention the diseases they might be reintroducing to past civilizations. So I took them all forward. Seemed safer."

"How far forward?"

"I didn't want you to ever have to worry about them," she said.

I repeated, "How far?"

She sipped her tea. "A thousand years."

I couldn't even fathom that. "You... you've seen what the planet will look like in a thousand years?"

"Sort of," she said, narrowing her eyes. "It's hard to explain. It would be like if Charlemagne popped up in the middle of Times Square. He would *see* it, but describing it to someone back home would be utterly impossible. They'd lock him up and call him a madman. So yes, I've seen it. And no, I'm not going to even try telling you anything about it."

There was no possible response to that, so I just watched her eat another spoonful of ice cream.

"So. You abandoned me because a cabal of rich pricks wanted to experiment on me to learn the secret of time travel. And when you were forced to raise me, you took those same pricks to the future and left them there."

"Mm-hmm."

"Jesus, Mom."

She shrugged and finished off the pint. She put it down on the table and folded her hands on the table. "People have only been time traveling for a few hundred years, as far as we can tell. And in that time, they figured out rules and guidelines to keep bad things from happening. Change too much, and eventually timelines crack under the weight of it all. There are journals about time travelers in the eighteenth century who went mad because they remembered six or seven different versions of their life. So they came up with rules."

"Rules that I was starting to break all over the place."

"It's my fault for not teaching you the do's and don'ts," she said. "Conspiring with yourself to rob banks is pretty high on the list. Purposefully creating separate timelines to cover up a crime, *also* very high. Might be the first thing, I'm not sure."

I said, "What about having sex with yourself?"

No, I don't know why I said that to my mother. I was in a very weird place, okay?

She shrugged. "Oh, sure. Everyone did that *all* the time."

I laughed and put my hands over my face. "I'm sorry I asked. No details. Please."

She chuckled and patted my hand.

I wondered how old the little version of me in the other room was. By which I mean, I wondered how much longer she would have a mother who hadn't vanished. I wanted to warn her. I wanted to ask, even hypothetically, why a time traveler might just never return from a trip. The answer was obvious. And tragic. Seeing her now, and with my new memories of her as a real mother, I knew she would never have chosen to leave me. So the only reason for her not coming back...

"You look like you're thinking very hard about something you don't want to think about at all."

I raised an eyebrow at her. "You read me well."

"I'm your mother. Whatever it is, don't tell me."

"I know," I said. "I'm done trying to change the future. And I think I can accept there are some questions I might never have an answer to."

The truth was, no matter when I lost her, it would be too soon. So instead of saying anything, I just stood up and opened my arms. She stood as well and stepped into a hug.

"I love you, Mom."

"I love you too, Chloe."

We held each other tightly, her head barely reaching my shoulder. I smiled and vowed that I wouldn't be the one to let go. Who knew how many more hugs we had left? Why cut any of them short?

"Mommy?"

She and I both turned toward the hallway. A teeny tiny version of me was standing there, mostly hidden by the wall with her head poking around. Her eyes were half-closed, and her hair was already a tangled mess from the brief time it had been on the pillow.

"Hey, sweetheart." Mom got up and went to her. "Were we being loud?"

Teeny tiny me nodded and rubbed her eyes. "Who's she?"

"That's a friend of mine. She just needed to ask me a question."

"Yeah," I said. "I was just about to leave. I, um, ate your ice cream."

"That's okay." Tiny Me let my mom pick her up. She twisted to look at me over Mom's shoulder. "You're pretty."

I smiled. "Thanks. So are you."

Mom patted the little girl's back. "I'm going to put her back to sleep. You'll be gone when I get back?"

She said it like a question, but it really wasn't. "Yeah. But before you go... that thing you mentioned. About taking someone with you. You're *positive* that's safe? Someone who... can't... go there by themselves? You could have brought them back safe if you wanted?"

"Sure," she said. "Whatever you have physical contact with will go with you. They were fine when they got there. Losing their damn minds, of course, but physically healthy. I did other tests later. It's as safe for them as it is for us."

"Okay. Good to know."

"What are you planning?"

I smiled and shrugged. "Right now, nothing. Just gathering information. Good night, Chloe."

She made a soft mumbling noise and burrowed deeper

into Mom's shoulder. Mom mouthed, 'be careful, Chloe,' and turned to take her daughter back to bed.

When they were gone, I left the apartment as quietly as possible.

Chapter Eighteen

I didn't push Stephanie. I didn't flood her phone with texts, I didn't show up at her apartment, I didn't do anything that might be construed as clingy. Oh, I *wrote* the texts. I got on the train and almost got off at her stop. I never tried going to where she worked, because she worked at a school, and a childless adult hanging around a school is a quick way to a lot of trouble. So that part was, at least, easy. Everything else was a trial. I grabbed my phone every time I got a notification, held my breath every time it rang, sure that this time it would be her, breaking her silence.

It wasn't her. For ten full days, none of the sounds made by my phone were her. I admitted I was starting to lose faith. The self-preservation part of my brain was preparing the other parts for the inevitable heartbreak.

On the eleventh day, a Friday, I got home to find Stephanie sitting on the floor next to my apartment door. The feelings that swelled in my chest proved my brain was a liar. I wasn't ready for this to be over. And if the final nail was about to be driven into our relationship, then I knew the pain would be legendary. I wanted to be with her. I wanted her in my life. Panic and pre-grief swarmed in my brain and strangled me, and a whole monologue of emotional vulnerability fought to get out of my mouth.

"Oh," I said out loud. "Hey."

Stephanie raised her eyebrows, looking bemused. "You're lucky I saw that deer-in-the-headlights look when you first spotted me. Because otherwise? Getting 'oh, hey,' after nearly two weeks of the cold shoulder? That would've been kind of brutal."

I clenched my jaw and stood up straighter. "Well. It serves you right. Because the past two weeks have been pretty brutal for me, too. Even though it was my fault."

Stephanie unfolded her legs and started trying to get up. I held out my hand to help her, and she gave me a quiet, 'thanks' in reply. She brushed off the seat of her pants and looked at the door. Then she looked at me.

"Should we go inside?"

"Is this going to be an 'inside' conversation?" I said.

She looked down the hall. "I... generally don't like having any personal conversations standing in a public hallway when there are chairs and a couch nearby." She realized what I was actually asking. "Oh. It's not going to be a fight."

I relaxed. "Okay. Then we can go inside." I took out my keys and let us into the apartment. "So how have you been?"

"Confused. Conflicted. Angry, for a little while, I guess." She walked past me and sat down on the couch. I liked how comfortable she was in my place. People who are about to dump someone don't get comfortable, right? "I never thought I'd have to think about my feelings on bank robberies as it pertains to my girlfriend. I never even really understood what happens to people's bank accounts if their bank is robbed."

"FDIC." I sat down in the armchair, instead of sitting next to her like I wanted. Giving her space.

"Right. I googled. That makes sense. I see it all the time so I never really considered what it meant. So when you took the money, no one lost their life savings or anything like that."

"Yeah. I did the research on that, too. I wanted to make

sure I wasn't ruining anyone's life."

Stephanie nodded. "I should've figured you would have considered that."

I linked my fingers together and waited. She scratched her cheek.

"I'm never going to do it again, by the way," I said.

"Oh. I figured that was a given. Thank you for saying it anyway."

"Yeah. In fact... I've spent a lot of time thinking these past few days. And I think I'm going to stop time traveling altogether."

Stephanie finally looked directly at me. "What? I'm not asking you to do that."

"No, of course not. You would never. But..." I pressed my lips together, then stood up and moved to kneel in front of her. "I don't know how old I am. Not exactly. Because I go back in time, I hang out there, I revisit happy memories. Sometimes my days are thirty hours long. Sometimes I have six weeks in one month. I spend so much time looking backward that the present just feels like a... a home base that I have to visit once in a while. It's not a home. It's not somewhere I have roots. Despite the fact I have a home and a job here. Before I met you, I didn't feel like I belonged in any specific time period because I could be whenever I wanted, for as long as I wanted. But now, I want to be here. I don't want to waste a single second somewhere else when I could be spending it with you."

Stephanie was smiling. She reached out and took my hands. "You're kind of stepping all over the speech *I* was planning to make."

"Oh god. I'm sorry. I—"

"No, don't be sorry." She laughed and leaned forward to kiss me. "I liked your speech better. Mine... the summary of mine is that I decided I could forgive you for making a mistake, but I couldn't forgive myself for letting you go. I like you a lot, Chloe. I like how relaxed you make me feel. I think this could go somewhere special. I'm not going to throw it away on a crime that technically happened decades ago where no one was hurt."

My heart wouldn't slow down. I was seriously a little concerned, but too distracted by hope to care. I squeezed her fingers.

"So we're... we can..." I swallowed the lump in my throat. "We're still together?"

She smiled. "Of course we are, Chloe."

I kissed her. I wrapped my arms around her and pushed her further back onto the couch so I could climb up onto her lap, straddling her. She laughed into the kiss and flattened her hand in the small of my back to pull me closer. It started as a celebratory kiss, but then my body realized Stephanie was underneath it again, for the first time in eleven long days, and it realized she was touching me and I was touching her. I melted against her as the tone of our kiss changed and became more passionate.

"I haven't showered," I whispered against her mouth.

"That's okay," she said. "I love your chef's uniform..."

"I know you do." I moved my lips to her ear, kissing the whole way. "I was never punished for robbing the bank."

Her fingers curled into a fist against my back. "Is that so," she said.

"Yes, ma'am."

She slid her hand down and went flat against the curve of my ass. She smoothed the material of my pants with her palm. I braced my arms on her shoulders and arched my back so I could look down at her, biting my lip, tense with anticipation.

"I wonder what the proper punishment for that should be..."

"I'm sure you'll think of someth~"

My words were cut off my yelp as she smacked my ass. I grinned and squirmed against her, grinding down onto her lap.

"We should move this somewhere else where you can be properly punished."

I leapt up and grabbed her hand, already unbuttoning my shirt with my other hand as I dragged her down the hall to the bedroom.

***

My ass was so sore I had to lay on my side afterward. Worth it. *So* worth it. Besides, it gave me a chance to cuddle up next to her and run my hand over her body, refamiliarizing myself with the bits that had almost faded from my mind during our time apart.

"I don't think I was ever going to leave you," she whispered. "I'm sorry I made you think that was a possibility. I just needed time to get used to the idea of... of everything."

"I understand," I said. "And I would have understood if you decided it was a dealbreaker. But honestly, it's not something I'd ever done before or would do again. It was such a damn headache." I sighed and shook my head.

Stephanie snickered. "So you're not going to commit a crime because it's too much of a hassle?"

"There are worse reasons to not commit crimes."

She laughed, we kissed, other things happened. I don't have to reveal every single thing. But it was a nice, energetic few minutes that ended with us swapping sides of the bed.

"So," I said, breathless, "there's something else."

"Oh, no."

"No, it's good. I promise." I propped myself up on my elbow so I could look down at her. "I went to visit my mother. We talked about a lot of stuff, but the part that you'll find interesting is that I learned I *can* take someone with me when I travel."

Stephanie blinked in surprise. "Oh wow."

"So. I know I just promised I'm going to stop traveling as much. Focus on now, build a foundation in the present. And I'm definitely going to do that. But I did some research..." I trailed my finger between her breasts. "Bowie did three nights in Chicago in 2004."

She sat up so quickly she almost knocked into my chin. "He had a heart attack backstage during that tour. Not here... I don't think. I don't know which show it was. But it ended up being his final tour." She cupped my face in her hands.

"Are you serious? Can you take me to see Bowie?"

I smiled and nodded as much as her hands would allow me. "If you want me to."

She kissed me hard, and I wrapped my arms around her, both of us falling back onto the bed.

"This is like a reward for forgiving you," she said. "Don't get me wrong. Just being with you is enough. I came back for *you*, and you alone. But this is a nice bonus."

I laughed. "I get it. I looked up the concerts, and there are sites that have the full playlist--"

"No, no, no, no, stop. No. Don't tell me. I don't want to know."

"Okay."

She said, "Sorry. It's just the surprise--"

"No, I get it," I said. "No spoilers."

"Thank you." She thought for a second and then said, "Does he play 'Heroes' at the one we're going to see...?"

I nodded. "He does."

"That's all I need to know. So? When are we going?"

"Whenever you want," I said with a shrug. "2004 is always going to be there."

"Wow. Okay. I'll find a spot in my schedule." She kissed me again. "Thank you. This is the most amazing thing anyone has ever done for me. Thank you."

"You're welcome. I'm glad I waited to do this. Like I said, it's been at the back of my mind forever, but I never got around to it."

She said, "No, it makes sense. You said it yourself. You don't go see Bowie alone. You go see Bowie..." She caught herself, gave a little breathy laugh, and touched the tip of my nose. "You go see Bowie with someone special."

Even if she was just repeating what I'd said to her, I had to admit the woman made a good point.

***

"Are you ready?"

"I don't know."

Stephanie looked down at herself for another once-over. She was wearing a sheer maroon blouse over a black tank top, tight black jeans, and a wide belt. We'd looked at pictures online from the era to get some idea of what people might be wearing and get some idea of the makeup situation. We eventually decided it was a Bowie concert, and it would be very difficult to look like a weirdo there. I was wearing a vintage shirt from a concert in the nineties and a pair of baggy jeans.

"What are you more nervous about?" I asked. "The concert or the time traveling?"

"Both." She laughed and pushed her bangs off her forehead. "I barely slept at all last night. And I've been buzzing about this all day. In a few minutes, it's going to be twenty years ago. Bowie's still going to be alive. And we're going to see him sing 'Heroes.' It's a lot to take in."

I nodded. "I guess I kind of got used to it after a while." I stepped closer and took her hands in mine. "Mom said I had to maintain physical contact with the person I want to travel with."

She stepped closer and placed her feet on the outside of mine. "How close do we have to be?"

I wrapped my arms around her waist. "Probably shouldn't risk it."

"Makes sense." She looked around the apartment. "Will you warn me before it happens?"

"Stephanie?"

"Mm-hmm?"

"We've still got to take the bus. And the train. If we jumped now, we would probably arrive in this apartment back in 2004, and I didn't live here then."

She said, "Oh. I thought we were... Then why are we already holding onto each other like this?"

"I don't need a reason to hold onto you."

"Flirt." She kissed my lips, then swatted my ass. "I can't believe I have to ride the train looking like a refugee from the nineties."

I took out my phone. "Would you rather take a Lyft?"

"Kind of."

So we called a car. The best thing about those drivers is that if you cut off conversation early, they usually don't bug you about the way you're dressed or why you're going to a theater where no events are currently scheduled. It had been a week since we... we... reunited? We didn't get back together because there'd been no breakup. Anyway, we'd been planning for a week. Stephanie was holding my hand so tightly I thought she would cut off the circulation to my fingers.

Two nights ago, I had tested my ability to carry living things through time. I'd found a cockroach in the alley behind my building. Grabbing it was the most disgusting thing I'd ever done, or at least in the running for top five. And I had to be very careful not to crush it and ruin the experiment. Once it was scurrying on my hand - ugh - I jumped back to a random date. 1997. The vile demon continued moving, so I jumped back home.

Then I had to keep the fucking thing in a box on my counter for twenty-four hours to make sure there weren't any lingering effects.

Then I took it outside and let it go, because I didn't know how to keep a cockroach alive, and I didn't want to mistake natural causes for a time travel-related death. He had survived both trips. I had to take that as confirmation of what Mom told me.

I squeezed Stephanie's hand. She laughed and jogged her leg up and down. "This is so exciting."

"I know," I said.

The driver glanced in the rearview mirror but didn't say anything.

It was a little after sunset when we got to the theater. There was a parking garage across the street, and I led Stephanie inside. We walked to a far corner on the lower level and I turned to look at her.

"Ready?"

She was out of breath. "Yeah. Let's go."

I wrapped my arms around her. She bracketed my feet with hers. I pressed my face into her shoulder. I could feel her shaking.

"Relax," I whispered.
"Will I feel it when it happens?"
I said, "You tell me."
She pulled back. "What? I don't know what..."
Her voice trailed off as she realized we were now surrounded by parked cars. Her jaw slowly dropped open as she realized it was earlier in the day than it had been a moment ago. Her hands went to my arms and gripped them tight.
"What..."
I chuckled and said, "Hey, Stephanie."
She looked at me.
"Welcome to 2004."

Chapter Nineteen

There was a moment when I thought that Mom was wrong, that my gross bug experiment had been useless. Stephanie's eyes were wide, but she didn't seem to be seeing anything. Her lips were moving but no sounds came out. She was shaking so violently I wanted to lay her down so she wouldn't fall, but the only available surface was the dirty concrete ground of the garage.

I risked lightly slapping her cheek a few times. "Stephanie? Honey, look at me. Look at me."

Focus returned to her eyes and she locked onto me. She pressed her lips together. She swallowed something that seemed to be the size of a peach pit, then blinked.

"This is 2004?"

I looked around. "I don't see any newspapers or signs or anything," I said, "but I almost never miss. Of course traveling with someone might~"

She cut me off with a kiss. I clung to her and kissed her back.

When she finally let me go, she said, "I just traveled in time."

"Yeah, you did. Are you okay? Any nausea or...?"

"Should I feel nauseated?"

"No." I tried to remember if I used to get queasy when I started. Maybe I had just gotten used to it over the years. "I don't think so. But do you~"

"No, I feel fine. I feel... I feel tingly. I don't think that's part of it."

I said, "No, I think that's just excitement."

"Adrenaline."

"Yeah." I brushed my thumb over her cheek. "Do you need a moment?"

Stephanie took a breath and then shook her head. "I'm okay. I'm fine. Walking will help. Can I lean on you?"

"Always."

I looped my arm around hers and guided her back toward the exit. She seemed to be doing fine until we got outside. Her grip tightened and she frantically scanned the area.

"Buildings are missing."

"I know," I said softly. "I know. They haven't been built yet."

She grunted, nodded, and then closed her eyes. "You really do this all the time?"

"Yeah. I learned to ignore the really freaky stuff."

"Okay. I'm good again."

I made sure she was steady before we started walking again. "I have to confess one thing. It's relatively small, it'll be fine, but I want you to be prepared."

"Oh no."

"No, it's... it'll be fine. It's just that I sort of promised I would stop messing with time. To my mother, and also to myself. So I couldn't just buy a ticket. It's a sold-out show, and any ticket I bought would be taking it away from whoever bought it in the original timeline. So this is his first night. We're going to try the cancelation window. We're going to look for scalpers. And if we come up empty, we'll just try tomorrow night. And if we come up empty then, we'll go all-out for the third night. You are *not* missing this concert."

She said, "Oh. Okay. I guess I can understand that. But..." She swallowed again. "We might have to time travel again?"

"Just twenty-four hours. It'll be fine. You'll be fine."

Stephanie shuddered and held tighter to my arm.

As I suspected, we fit in completely with the rest of the attendees outside the Rosemont Theater. There were enough people our age for us to go unnoticed as we made our way to the cancelation window.

"Cross your fingers," I whispered.

The tuxedoed girl behind the glass smiled as we approached. It was the smile of someone who knew what we were going to ask and was ready to give good news. Or at least that's how I interpreted it. We arrived at the window and, a second later, I was vaguely aware of someone stepping into line behind us, but there was enough of a crowd that I barely registered them.

"Hi," I said, "we're hoping you have two tickets available."

The girl's smile widened. "You're in luck!"

Stephanie tightened her grip. "This is really happening."

I beamed and handed over the cash, and the girl passed two tickets under the window. I thanked her and stepped aside so the people behind us could move forward.

"Sorry," the girl in the tuxedo said. "Those were the last two tickets."

I stopped and looked back. Did that count as changing history? Making a new timeline? Had we gotten tickets those two were supposed to get? The guy looked to be in his mid-twenties with a receding hairline and muscles that stretched the sleeves of his jacket. Something about him was familiar to me, but I couldn't place him. The girl with him seemed bored, scanning the crowd with eyes that didn't really see anything. In a few years, she would have been mindlessly scrolling through her phone, but for now she was stuck people-watching.

The balding guy looked at me like I'd just picked his pocket. Which, to be fair, I had. Stephanie had been watching him, and she glanced at me.

"Chloe...?"

"It's okay," I said.

The girl bumped his arm. "Come on, Darwin, we tried. Let's just go do something else. There's just a bunch of old people here."

When he turned to grimace at her, I suddenly realized where I knew him from. I was stunned enough to ignore her 'old people' comment. Sixteen years ago. A street corner. This motherfucker punched me in the face.

"This is *Bowie*!" Darwin said to his date. "Do you know how much cred I'll get for seeing him live? Jordan will piss himself, he'll be so upset!"

"Cred?" I laughed and looked at Stephanie. "Did people still say 'cred' in 2004?"

Darwin stepped closer. "Listen, bitch. Just hand over the tickets."

Okay. I already knew this douchebag was the kind of guy who would hit a stranger, a *woman*, in the face over something that had happened - in his experience - four years earlier. But it was nice of him to give me another reason to want to screw him over.

"Sorry, Darwin," I said. "Maybe you should've left the house a little earlier. Or planned ahead. Also? You don't see Bowie because you think it'll make you look cool in front of your friends. You see him because he's David fucking Bowie. If you don't understand that, you don't deserve the tickets."

He moved even closer. I could smell his breath. "I'll give you one last chance..."

"Babe." The girl sounded horribly bored now. She was already drifting away. "Let's go-o-ah." She did that thing where she turned 'go' into multiple syllables with a lilt at the end.

Darwin glared at me for another few seconds, then jabbed his finger at me. "If I ever see you again..."

"Yeah, yeah," I said. "I'm prepared for that. Worth it."

He finally let his hand drop and stepped away. He followed the girl through the crowd, turning back to look at me a few times on his way to the door. I watched him as well, not giving him the satisfaction of turning away. I heard Stephanie let out a breath of relief, then felt her hand on my shoulder.

"Do you really think he's going to let it go?"

"No," I said. "In four years, he's going to see me on the street and punch me in the face."

"*What?*"

I looked at her and shrugged. "It was more scary than anything. I got a nosebleed. But on the bright side, it means that this is all happening in our timeline anyway. I don't have to worry about the tickets fucking anything up. That almost makes it worth getting punched in the face."

Stephanie laughed awkwardly. "Okay, then." She examined my face. She pinched my nose and wiggled it, as if she was checking to make sure it was still intact. "If you've already suffered for it, I'm not going to waste time worrying."

"Smart." I offered her my arm. "Shall we find our seats?"

She slipped her arm around mine and pulled me close. "Let's."

***

The Thin White Duke leaned close to the microphone. "You're not too old for a sing-along, are ya?" he asked with a sly smile. The audience cheered. "Heh heh heh. Yeah well, let's see..." He stepped back and the band swung straight into "All the Young Dudes."

We'd been on our feet ever since the concert started, with everyone around us scream-singing "REBEL REBEL" along with the band. Stephanie had immediately become half her age, dancing as wildly and singing as loudly as any of the actual twenty year olds in the room. She wasn't the only one who seemed to be defying the passage of time. Bowie himself was dressed in a long tattered coat and an ascot, looking like a down-on-his-luck pirate. He strutted and danced on the stage, and his ability to hold a note at a volume that shook the rafters was truly incredible.

The singer might have been in the spotlight, but I only had eyes for Stephanie. She quickly proved herself to be the far superior fan between the two of us, singing along even to the deepest cuts (who the hell knows all the words to "Fall Dog Bombs the Moon," I mean *seriously*. Even the people around us didn't know it because, for them, it was a brand-new release).

She was smiling so big, and for so long, it was starting to hurt *my* face. She danced, she sang along, she cheered and whooped loud enough that I was sure Bowie heard her above everyone else. When the opening chords of "Life on Mars?" started, Stephanie grabbed my hand and leaned in close enough to be heard over the cheers.

"I know I said 'Heroes,' but *this* is the song I most wanted to hear." She pressed her lips to my cheek. "Thank you. *Thank you.*"

I kissed her back, then joined her (and about four thousand other people) in singing along. It was probably one of my favorites of his, too. I definitely liked it more than 'Heroes.'

After two hours, I think we were both more exhausted than the man we'd come to see. He never missed a beat, never seemed breathless, and performed the final songs with the same energy he'd started the night with. I never would have guessed it was his last tour. I remembered what Stephanie had told me. A heart attack during one concert, taken away by an ambulance, and then no new music for a decade. Then two more albums, and... the end.

I looked around the room at the other fans. Young kids who had just discovered his music. Older fans who had been there from the beginning. None of them knew how lucky they were to be here on this night, with such a legend.

Well. One of them knew.

I reached for Stephanie's hand. She looked at me, smiled, and then leaned in to kiss me.

"I love you," I said.

She blinked in surprise, then smiled, laughed and leaned down next to my ear. "Say it again."

I pressed my lips to her cheek. "I love you."

"I love you, too," she said at the exact moment the band

started playing "Heroes."

And we kissed.

***

The show ended with "Ziggy Stardust," and the crowd kept cheering long after Bowie left the stage. When we all had to finally admit the night was over, the whole mass of us started moving toward the exits. I started toward the aisle, but Stephanie squeezed my hand and shook her head. I came back to her and we both sat down in the seats we'd been neglecting most of the night. The room was still buzzing with energy, almost as if the echoes of the music were caught in the corners and still bouncing back and forth.

"That was... amazing. Literally awesome, in the original sense of the word. I can't believe I just saw that. I can't believe you gave this night to me. It's the most amazing thing anyone's ever done for me. Thank you, Chloe."

"You're very welcome. I don't think it would've been anywhere near as fun on my own. I'm glad I got to experience it with you."

She held out her hands toward the stage. "I just heard David Bowie sing 'Heroes.' I can't believe it."

"I always thought that was a sad song. Or tragic, at least. Nothing will keep them together. Nothing will help them."

Stephanie said, "It's not tragic at all. It's a call to action. Nothing will keep them together, so they have to do it themselves. Nothing's going to help. No one is going to swoop in and save the relationship. It's all up to them. And you heard how he was singing it. He's up for the challenge. He's willing to fight. They'll be heroes by saving themselves."

I drew in a deep breath and let it out slowly. "Wow. Okay. You officially changed my mind on the song."

She laughed and leaned in to kiss my cheek.

I cleared my throat. "And, um. I feel like there was something else toward the end...? Right before the encores... I think you said something?"

She furrowed her brow. "Did I? Wow. It's so hard to hear anything in here."

"Maybe I was hearing things."

"I wouldn't be surprised," she said. "Very easy to mistake, you know... speaker feedback for your girlfriend saying 'I love you' for the first time."

"I hear it happens constantly."

She looked at me and smiled. "I love you, Chloe."

"I love you, too, Stephanie."

"Do we have to go home right away? I feel like I could run all the way there."

I laughed. "The sign of an excellent concert. No, we don't have to do anything right away. I can take us back to seconds after we left, if you want."

She shook her head. "No. This needs to have taken real time. At least three hours. However long we spend here, that's how much time I want to have passed."

"We can do that. It makes sense. And it doesn't fuck with your age."

"You really don't know how old you are?" she said.

I shrugged. "I'm not saying there are years' worth of difference. But yeah, my birthday isn't an exact target. Some years are longer than others. So while I was born thirty-three years ago, there's a chance I could be thirty-four."

"Dating you is so weird."

"But worth it."

She grinned. "Even without the once in a lifetime concert experiences."

I looked at her. "Who said anything about 'once'...?"

She looked at me and raised an eyebrow, intrigued.

Chapter Twenty

We ended up leaving the theater a few minutes later. We walked for a long time, no destination in mind. I told Stephanie it didn't matter since we could jump home from anywhere, so we might as well enjoy the stars. We weren't very far from O'Hare, so occasionally we got to see some low-flying planes coming in for a landing or heading out into the night sky. We made a game of trying to guess where each one was going to or coming from.

"So," Stephanie said, "are you still going to stop living in the past?"

"I'm going to try."

She nodded slowly, thoughtfully. "I understand that. And now that I've actually experienced it, I also understand the appeal. Coming back here with the benefit of hindsight? Those people probably knew they saw an amazing show. They'll remember it forever just based on that. But only we know how close it is to the end. We're the only ones who appreciated it as a swan song, and I think that's beautiful."

"Yeah," I said. "It can be emotional."

She moved to stand in front of me. "Don't stop traveling.

Maybe be a little more thoughtful about where you go, and maybe restrict it to once a month or something. But you've been given an amazing gift. You shouldn't squander it just because you were getting addicted. The past is... *memory* is a precious thing. Don't waste it."

"I might need help monitoring it. Someone to make sure I don't go overboard." I tilted my head to the side. "Know anyone who might be interested?"

She pretended to think. "Well... if I'm not mistaken, you said I'm the only person who knows?"

"Right."

"That kind of narrows down the pool of candidates."

I said, "You have a point. So. You want the job?"

She moved back to my side and looped her arm through mine again. "Can we go on other trips like this?"

"We'd have to," I said. "As my supervisor, you'd need to actually observe me and make sure I only went on approved jumps."

"I suppose that's a small price to pay for great sex."

"I'm paying you in sex?"

"Yes."

"Good thing you're the one who got the job."

She laughed and used her arm to pull me closer. I had actually always hated walking arm-in-arm with people. It had always felt like an anchor before. Dragging someone along, forced to move at their pace. Earlier, I had done it with Stephanie because she was so shaky and uncertain on her feet. But now, I had to admit I definitely saw the appeal.

"So," I said, focusing on the sidewalk ahead of us. "I'll have the paperwork drawn up when we get home. The best thing about being my employee is you get an advance on your first paycheck."

"Sounds perfect," Stephanie said. "Where else have you always wanted to go?"

I thought for a second. "Well, now that I know I can jump outside my lifetime~"

"Is that not a rule?"

"No, that's from *Quantum Leap*."

"Oh, right. I loved that show."

I laughed. "I've always wanted to see the Chicago Shrikes win the World Series."

"First women's team," she said. "Excellent choice. 1914 or something?"

"Around then." I looked at her. "So what do you think, Coach Keith? Want to go see a baseball game?"

She laughed and pretended to check her wrist for a watch. "Tonight? I don't know, I feel like it's already been a pretty full evening."

"It doesn't have to be tonight," I said. "Whenever you want. We've got all the time in the world."

***

So that's the story of why a stranger named Darwin punched me in the face in 2008, because of something I did in 2004, which I didn't know about until 2024. I know I took some detours. But it really wouldn't have made sense without going through the whole thing. I had to explain who Stephanie was, and to explain her, I had to explain why I was returning from the Great Chicago Fire, and I could only explain that by explaining the bank heist.

Fine. Maybe I rambled a little.

Things were mostly calm after all that settled down. Stephanie and I ended up taking trips together once a month or so, depending on if we could think of somewhere we really wanted to go. We did end up seeing the Chicago Shrikes play. We ended up attending quite a few games, actually, and Stephanie got an autograph from Caroline Rainey that's probably worth a couple grand to a collector. Of course the provenance would be kind of hard to explain if we did ever want to sell it.

Stephanie and I moved in together six months after the Bowie concert. It was the perfect way to discover all the little ways she could get on my nerves and all the bad behavior she had (there was nothing for her to discover about me, I'm perfect, she's just nitpicky). Even better, it was a good way to learn that those things didn't matter. I wanted to be with her, and she wanted to be with me, warts and all.

On a Wednesday afternoon when I was off but Stephanie had to coach, I took a little trip to the future. But not our future. See, I had cut way back on my traveling, but I still did a solo jaunt now and again. It was easy to keep my promise to Stephanie because it was much less fun going alone now that I had a sidekick. But sometimes I visited Mom and we talked about how to use my ability. So when I visited the future on that Wednesday afternoon, I didn't go to our future.

I went to see the Dame.

She was still living in the same apartment I had in 2024, the place I'd already left behind to cohabitate with Stephanie in "neutral ground." I arrived while she was at work, but the doorman was criminally unsuspicious of me when I asked if he could let me into her apartment as a surprise.

"Never knew Missus Cross had a daughter," he said, twisting back to look at me.

"She's a real enigma," I said.

He snickered and nodded, then wished me a good day. I went inside and sat on her couch to wait until she showed up.

The Dame was expecting me when she arrived. The doorman must have ruined the surprise.

"What are you doing here?" she asked, dropping her purse and keys.

"I wanted to talk."

"If you want to try another heist—"

I shook my head. "No. No interest in wasting anyone's time like that." I looked at her uniform jacket. "What's Otenba?"

"My restaurant. Dutch-Japanese fusion."

I raised my eyebrows. "That sounds... interesting."

"How long has it been since the heist?" she asked, cutting off any further small talk.

"About six months. The FN Phantom stuff is still a headache, but I'm learning to live with it. Consequences of my actions. It could've been a lot worse."

She nodded and went to the kitchen. She retrieved a beer

from the fridge and came back without offering me one.

"So why are you here?"

"Because I wanted to confirm something. Another version of me said you were the mastermind behind the whole heist plot. You acted like you were just trying to clean up the mess I made with Neighbor - who I know you claim to have never met - but I think she was telling the truth. You had years to come up with the plan. I don't know why you needed me to do it for you~"

"Buffering," she said. "It was obvious there would be consequences for what I wanted to do. I thought if you were the one who actually did the robbery, you'd suffer instead of me."

I laughed. "Wow. You really are a massive asshole."

She smiled and held her arms out to the side. "See you in a couple of years."

"No," I said. "Because I realized why you came up with the idea in the first place. It's because you're from a timeline where you never met Stephanie."

She narrowed her eyes. "Who?"

"Oh." I took a step back and put a hand to my chest. "Wow. I did not expect that to hurt. Wow." I cleared my throat and collected myself. "Stephanie Keith. She's a PE teacher and she coaches soccer. When she gets her hair cut too short, she looks like a mouse. She has a daughter named Jessica. She likes rough sex and David Bowie and if you leave Oreos on the counter, she *will* demolish them even if you're saving them for later."

The Dame's face had turned to stone. "She sounds lovely."

"She is," I said. "She's going to be my wife."

The Dame looked as surprised as I felt. I hadn't realized I was going to say that, but I didn't need to be a time traveler to know I was telling the truth.

"And if I'd never met her... and I was still here at your age, on my own, I think I would've done something drastic to create some excitement in my life."

"I'm not alone," she said. "I date. I have people."

I shrugged. "I'm sure you do. I don't think you're sad or even depressed. I think you just want something more. Who can blame you? You spent your entire life in the past. Thinking about where and when you could go, what you could do without consequences. You never thought about the future. You never thought about..." I gestured vaguely at the apartment. "This."

"I'm happy with 'this'."

"Sure you are. I've only known Stephanie for half a year, but I already dread the thought of going back to the way life was before. And no offense, but I am *immensely* glad to know I don't have to worry about ending up like you."

The Dame said, "Unless she leaves you. Shit happens. I haven't been alone this whole time. There have been..." She looked down at the floor and drummed her fingers on the side of the bottle. "You look at me and you see a worst case scenario. And you can't *imagine* a world where the happiness you're here bragging about goes away. Maybe I had that once. Not with this Stephanie person, but I've had it. And losing it...? You can't see how that might contribute to you turning into this?"

"Okay," I said. "So you're not a dodged bullet. You're a cautionary tale. I can work with that, but I'm not going to waste my time worrying about it. Every relationship takes work. And Stephanie is worth doing it, no matter how hard the work might be."

And I know, not that long ago I joked about how I was perfect. I retract that statement. I have a lot to work on and Stephanie's criticisms are justified.

Most of them, anyway.

"I'm going to stop living in the past. I'm not going to worry about the future. I'm ready to live in the present."

The Dame raised her bottle in a toast that seemed only partially sarcastic. "Well, here's to the happy couple. I think I'll skip the ceremony."

"Probably for the best." I walked to the door. "Have a nice life, Chloe."

"Hey," she said.

I stopped on the threshold and looked back at her. She was staring at the mouth of her bottle. "The work is never too hard. No matter how hard it might seem, if it gets you through and keeps her around, then it's never too hard. Remember that."

I nodded. "I will."

She raised her bottle again with even less sarcasm. I nodded in acknowledgement of the toast, then left her to whatever sort of life she'd built for herself.

***

I found Stephanie at the school's soccer field. She looked damn good in a red polo shirt and white shorts. She was wearing a visor and sunglasses to block the sun, but I still knew the moment she spotted me. She waved me over. I waited for her to kiss me first, since we were in public. It might have been 2024 and we were in a fairly liberal city, but there was always a chance some parent would make a fuss.

"Come to watch us lose?" she asked cheerfully.

"Oh, I'm sure you'll come through."

She laughed and crossed her arms, facing the field again. "Not this game. But it's fine. Losing teaches them things, too."

"Good philosophy."

She nodded. "So what's up?"

"Nothing's up. I just wanted to see you."

I had decided I was going to marry this woman. I'd made that decision, and I was confident she would say yes, and once both those facts were locked in, I wanted to see her as quickly as possible.

"Aw, that's sweet." She bent down and kissed my lips. "I promised the girls pizza after the game. You can join us, if you want. They've been begging to meet you."

"You've told them about me?"

She said, "Of course. They're nosy teenagers with romance fetishes. I bait them with information in exchange for doing drills."

I raised my eyebrows. "Oh wow, you're evil."

"I do what needs to be done." She looked at the field

again. "So? Pizza?"

"Sure. Pizza sounds great."

She nodded and we watched the game for a bit.

"They really are getting destroyed out there."

Stephanie laughed. "Sh. Don't let anyone hear you say things like that."

"I'll be good."

"Good. Just stand there and look pretty."

I laughed and mock-slapped her arm.

I was going to ask this woman to marry me. And she would say yes. Then we would plan a wedding, which we would then execute, and then she would be my wife. I was so excited I could hardly wait. But I would wait. Even though I could very easily just jump ahead to the aftermath, I wouldn't do that. I would live through each long, agonizing day to earn the reward at the end of the road.

Some things were very much worth waiting for.

ABOUT THE AUTHOR

Geonn Cannon is the author of over sixty novels, including the Riley Parra series which was adapted into an Emmy-nominated webseries by Tello Films. His novel *Can You Hear Me* was adapted into *Static Space*, an award-winning short film. He's also written two tie-in novels for the television series *Stargate SG-1*. He was the first male author to win a Golden Crown Literary Society Award for his novel *Gemini*, and he won a second for *Dogs of War*.